Redeemed by a Rake

by

Susan Payne

Cover Art by *Teddi Black*

The Wild Rose Press, Inc.
PO Box 708
Adams Basin, NY 14410-0708
Visit us at www.thewildrosepress.com

Publishing History
First Edition, 2025
Trade Paperback ISBN 978-1-5092-6318-9
Digital ISBN 978-1-5092-6319-6

Published in the United States of America

Dedication

To my family who have always supported me in so
many ways.

CHAPTER ONE

English Countryside
1808

"I can make you respectable again."

Startled hazel eyes stared back at him. The young woman Tony confronted in the garden of the small cottage off the village green captivated him. She had met him at her gate with a hesitant, but pretty smile showing even white teeth. Her skin was unblemished with a light sprinkling of freckles, testament to the time she spent outside, he was sure. She appeared younger than he knew her to be.

She must not have been expecting anyone since her golden-brown hair was tucked haphazardly under a mob cap, and the apron covering her lavender mourning dress was stained where she had been kneeling on the ground. He was sure there were work boots covering her feet under that same gown.

"Let me begin again. I am Viscount Wyndom, Anthony Randoff." He gave a slight bow although his eyes remained staring directly into the woman's seeking some response. Hoping for some recognition. There was none. "My mother is a good friend of Lady Winters, your godmother."

Those words seemed to calm her. "You brought a message for me? Is she well?"

"The last time the two of us spoke she was quite well, and although I do not bring a message as such, she thinks you should hear what I have to say."

The young woman remained silent, yet he could see his being there intrigued her. She had probably figured Lady Winters must have given him this cottage's directions for him to have found her in a simple village so far from where she belonged.

She tipped her head as if willing to listen without making any comment to do so. It was a start and a good one, he thought. Now to tell her what he wished without telling her more than she needed to know. It had seemed easier on the long drive from London than it did in this crowded walled garden.

He tried to seem accommodating. "May we ascend into the cottage? What I wish to discuss should be kept between the two of us, and we are right on the edge of the road."

Her gaze flicked between himself and the cottage door with her finally making up her mind to turn toward it leaving him to follow. Evidently, she also wished any business between them to be kept private.

He removed his hat and bent to enter the two-rooms she called home.

She turned quickly when she met the wall and stated rather bluntly, "Why have you come?"

"I am here to make you an offer for an alternate life."

He felt the rage radiate from her being as she inhaled deeply to tell him exactly what he could do with his offer. An offer she had completely misunderstood. He raised his hand to prevent her from damning him and his plans to perdition before he was able to make his case.

"You need to hear me out before making another

mistake in your young life. Lady Winters would not have allowed me access to you if she did not think my plan was the best offer for you to be reunited with those you love. To be accepted into society where you belong as the daughter of an earl."

Tony needed to overcome her doubts for his plan to work. The only thing this intelligent young woman would believe was the truth. And truth, no matter how unpalatable, was better than living with deceit and lies. Needing to always cover-up what was in your heart.

"I am offering you marriage."

Her head tipped toward him indicating interest in hearing him out although her expression was wary.

"Marriage to me would allow you to return to your friends and family, at least for short visits. I do not plan to have you live in London, but it seems as if you make your own entertainment in the country."

His gaze moved about the neat room with its knitting basket and paint stand. Lace hanging on wooden dowels.

"I do not understand. You wish to marry me? Why? I have no dowry to speak of, and you must know my history, my shame..."

"I have recently ascended to my title and as you can see am not in the throes of youth." He read the question in her eyes and answered, "I am three and thirty."

He waited for that fact to sink in before continuing. "I know you are from a good family with acceptable morals up to a certain point. I know that a girl's head can be turned by a handsome young man in uniform, and those same young men are sometimes under pressure to put more into their life since they face possible death."

She was trying to control her breathing. Her gaze travelled toward the still open door more often than he would like. As if she would run away if given half a chance to get past him.

"It was not like that. There was an attraction between us as soon as we met. It grew into so much more, and yet everyone said we could not be together. There was no time, and we were so desperate. He gave me a ring. We were betrothed even if everyone else thought differently. We were so in love…"

He did not wish her to focus on the past. He needed her to think about the future—her future and what he could offer.

"My mother is urging me to begin my family to ensure the title remains in the lineage. She feels she shall not live much longer and wishes to see me settled, knowing that I have an heir. Not that I think she shall die as soon as I furnish those things, but I know it is time, as well."

"So, what have you done to blacken your name so much you must scrounge up someone polite London has shunned and dispensed with long ago?"

"I, ah, nothing, yet." This would be the tricky part. This would make or break his future plans. "I have been living in Italy…with a lady who is not my wife and who refuses to become my wife."

"And why is that? Is she already married?"

It was a rude question, but he would rather she ask and know the truth than turn him away.

"She is a widow with her own funds and a few years older than I. She is also known to be barren, so there would be no chance of offspring. That fact had not bothered either of us although now it seems to be of importance. At least to my mother who is aware of my liaison."

The young woman nodded as if putting it all together, but to make sure, asked, "You wish me to marry you and be your wife here in England while you return to your lover in Italy?"

"Well, I probably could find a lady who would agree to that since I have the funds to make any woman's life easier and provide her with anything she may wish or desire. I need someone who would not wish to be in London society since I and my lady friend would be taking up residences there. There are not many new wives who would allow me such access to my mistress while remaining quietly at home bearing my children. Most women would try to take revenge by taking a lover of their own."

"I see. You wish for someone you can walk all over."

A slight smile raised one side of his mouth acknowledging the humor of her words. "No, please do not think of it in that manner. I was hoping we would both get what we wish from the marriage. You would be accepted as a properly married woman with a home and children while I lived a life with the woman I love and cannot abandon. We have been together for over eight years, and she is such a part of me. Certainly, long enough for any youthful fling to have run its course which is what everyone assured me it was. She understands my need for an heir, and we have discussed our moving to England for that to occur. I assure you no one shall be hurt in this arrangement as long as we all go into this with our eyes open."

Her head shook in the negative. "Lord Wyndom, I cannot agree to any of this. I have a life here and am content."

"Content is not happy."

A small grimace as the truth revealed itself. He pursued his advantage.

"Can you say you are happy? Would not some happiness return if you could write to past friends and relatives and know they would welcome the correspondence? That they would write letters in return? That you could walk down any street and not fear being shunned or cut directly? As my wife, you would hold a certain level of respect in my district. You would be expected to host certain village events, guide the vicar of whom I provide the living, work with a full staff of servants who shall answer to you as mistress of the house. You could manage the steward who runs the home-farm and oversees a dozen tenant farmers."

"You have a long list of benefits, but so far, they seem to center on me. Besides the heir and spare you desire, why me?"

"As I said, my mother knows your godmother, and Lady Winters is still quite a champion of your charms and abilities. I have been assured you are well qualified to run a household such as I have just described. She mentioned you are attractive, and I must concur with that summation. After all, no one wishes their children to be antidotes."

He smiled although he was not joking in the slightest. This was exactly the reasoning he used as his method to decide whether or not to ask for her hand.

"You have proven yourself to be fertile even if your first child did not live long. I have been convinced it was not an inherent problem with the child, but with the infant being too long denied air during its birth. I shall make sure, as my wife, you are surrounded by more than competent people for your lying-in. There is no reason not to expect a better result the next time."

Interrupting him, she said through gritted teeth. "Never refer to my child again, sir, or I shall not be liable for the damage I do you."

He hesitated a moment before apologizing. "I meant no offense. The fact you chose to confine yourself in the back of beyond and raise your child yourself instead of sending it to some tenant farmer to foster does you a justice in my eyes. It proved you had loyalty as well as honor just as you confessed the child's parentage thereby giving all parties a chance to lessen their grief through knowing the man's child."

"And what if the child had lived? Would you still find yourself in my garden presenting the same offer?" She sounded waspish. Her patience was truly diminished.

"Yes, and probably refer to a previous marriage which left you a widow. Much as what appeared to have happened."

Biting her lip, she nodded. "You are one of the few who understand what I tried to do when I first found I was with child. Lessen Christopher's parents' loss by offering his child to them in his place. The fact it was a boy should have helped them, but they refused to even admit the possibility that Christopher and I were betrothed or that their son could have left a grandchild behind. Admittedly a child he had not known about, but still a part of him. Part of Christopher and myself. I never thought about abandoning the infant to another family to raise as their own."

Tony thought he best change the subject before she ended-up wallowing in the past hurts.

"As my wife you would have a quarterly allowance to spend as you wish. All household and clothing expenses would be placed through the steward who acts as my man of business. I suppose I might get another for my London expenses, but that should not affect you or the country estate in the slightest. I have additional funds from my maternal grandfather."

Her question came as a relief and surprise since he had not thought she was still considering his offer. As if unbidden, the words came from her mouth.

"May I hire a personal maid? I had to let my own go when I moved here, and we had been close. She would need a cottage or something since she now has a family."

Hope leaped within him. If his plan was still viable, he would have granted her any request.

"I am sure Fellner, the steward, can find a place for her near the manor if you are sure, you will not need her during the night. I suppose it could work."

"Um, she is marvelous at taking care of lace and has a fine stitch that barely shows. I thought her a jewel when she worked for me."

His heart pounded in his chest. Was this the turning point he thought had passed him by? Was this young lady going to make his life in England possible as well as endurable?

"Then consider it a *fait accompli*. Do I take it that you are no longer denying me the possibility of accepting my proposition? I believe it shall have benefits to both of us, and I shall put some of it on paper as in a marriage contract. Of course, I do not wish people to think I am paying you to carry my children. I wish my progeny to have both a loving mother and father and be raised in as normal an environment as possible. There could be no talk that they are not my blood."

She spoke as if she had become a different woman. The intelligence Lady Winters boasted this young woman had begun to show itself. "I have no expectations of your time other than what it shall take to get with child which may not take long. You shall then be able to live anywhere you wish until after the child is born and a second child needed. I shall keep you updated with information so that you shall know how they go on."

Her briskness surprised him. "It sounds as if you have been making plans while we stood here. Your godmother said you were intelligent and good at managing. I appreciate your thinking I would wish to know how my offspring get on although I plan on visiting them even in their infancy. I do not wish to be a complete stranger when they come up to town for visits or during school holidays."

"I may have, my lord. I think we shall rub along quite well for the most part. I only ask that you not bring your, um, friend with you when you visit since village gossip is terribly intolerant of anything out of the norm. I would not wish your children to overhear and question their father's activities."

He narrowed his eyes trying to find any underlying reason for her request. "I do not think the two of you shall ever have a reason to meet. My friend is in agreement that this is the best method to accomplish what I must while keeping the relationship between her and I as strong as it has ever been."

****

Sarah made her decision. "Send me the papers with everything written out."

She did not know where she got the strength to

speak so firmly, but she knew an opportunity such as this would not come her way again. A woman who had borne an out-of-wedlock child would not be considered proper wife material for a titled man of wealth. This was going to make her other plans so much easier she did not dare think of them while still faced with the hard stare of her now future husband.

"Do you not wish to acquire the services of a solicitor of your own? It would normally fall to the lady's closest male kin."

"I assure you I am quite capable of reading and to speak for myself," she informed him, needing to reinforce her independence. She would do nothing that she was not in agreement with, and he would have no control other than what she gave him. Two could make-up rules to this sort of unusual arrangement.

As if just thinking of something, he said, "My mother, well anyone, must not know of our agreement. Other than the lawyers, it shall be between you and I, and I assure you I shall not allow anyone to question our marriage. After all, many *ton* marriages are for convenience only to join landholdings or wealth. Ours shall not be thought any different than that except you shall know going into the marriage where you stand. You shall not be hurt by my having another in my life. Unlike an untried debutant, you have known love and understand how it takes over even the most honorable of people."

"I assume the woman you are involved with shall know the truth about our agreement?"

"Of course. I would not wound her in such a manner. I would accompany you to the country until you are *enceinte* and then leave you to your life while I return to my townhouse in London. I plan to be discreet although others know of my interest in this other lady. She is of an age that it is acceptable for her and I to be together—again under the most discreet of conditions."

"While I rusticate in the country, my lord?" Sarah wondered how discreet he thought he would be allowed to be in the town the size of *tonish* London. Unless he wished to keep to the darker gambling hells and subscription balls, he shall find English nobility a hotbed of gossip and scandal.

"Is it any different than how you are living now? Except you shall not need to skip meals and wear made-over hand-me-down gowns."

She kept from brushing her mended skirt or noting in any manner he had hit a sore spot. "You have given me much to think about as you must realize. I shall not make such a decision so quickly. I too have a love I cannot abandon, and I am not sure a relationship such as you are offering would be good for a child. Any child. If there is anything I understand, it is how strong a mother's love is, and I shall not allow you to force me from my child or out of its life when you tire of our arrangement."

"I understand and would not put either you or the child in such a position. Remember this would bring you back into society which is still uncertain as to what actually happened. I know of such questions due to certain things I must keep private. But the requirements shall all be laid out in the marriage contract. I shall always provide a home for you as my wife and the mother of my children, and you shall have all the benefits of their mother as long as you do not embarrass me by taking lovers or living with another man. I shall protect my children from such scandal if at all possible."

Viscount Wayland bowed again and left her to think about what her future could be with this man's largess.

Sarah had enough to worry about without thinking what her life would be in years to come. Years from now when the viscount's need for a broodmare was over and their children were away in school or safely married.

Besides, Sarah knew her heart was buried in some graveyard in Spain with the man she had known for such a brief time.

Tears welled in her eyes. Oh, Christopher, my love, what have I done? I can see the benefits, but there are sure to be drawbacks to such an unloving arrangement. Can I allow another man to touch me after knowing how sweet your touch felt? Can I birth another man's child and feel the same love as I did for yours?

This morning had begun in so normal a manner, Sarah barely understood the opportunity when it presented itself. A means to have the future she planned when her son was born.

Of course, she had been aware there was a strange carriage in the village. Strange as in it did not belong to the large manor at the top of the hill and strange that it had not visited there first. No one who could afford such a rig ever came through Little Castleton since it was on the way to and from nowhere. One of the reasons she had chosen the small village in which to live. That and she could afford to rent the cottage since it had been in need of new waddle which her one-time lady's maid, Lucy, had her male friend mend. It had cost a few meals and an extra day off for Lucy, but was well worth it since Sarah had been tight and warm in the home ever since. That was coming on to two years now, and she was very well ensconced in the village and her life here. Having strange carriages coming and unsettling her was not something she welcomed. She had known she would not be at ease until it rolled out again.

Her mind had turned to the possible reasons it was visiting. It could be a solicitor seeking a villager or a magistrate to inform a villager of a death. Only those men usually went to the parish house first to collect the vicar. And, of course, it could be a tax collector although she found they drove around in equipage of a much lesser quality than the one she saw driving past with the coachman and postilion wearing matching liveries.

Whoever it was seemed to think highly of himself driving through with the draperies drawn to hide the occupants. No matter who they were or why they were there, Sarah would feel much less anxious if they would finish their business quickly and leave.

Returning to weeding the already neat garden, pulling those plants that were winding down in the cooler fall months, she failed to hear the man approach until he was opening the squeaky gate. A gate left to squeak specifically so she would know when anyone entered her domain. The only place she felt safe with her own thoughts.

The raven-haired man loomed over Sarah causing her to feel fear for her safety for the first time in Little Castleton. He wore a greatcoat with several capes to repel inclement weather. The curled brimmed top hat along with fur-lined leather gloves were more than adequate on what most would consider a mild fall day. The tan of his face belied his manner of dress since he must brave the wind and sun on his skin at some point. The deeper color of his face only made the piercing blue eyes more striking and the wide mouth showed neither happiness at finding her nor disapproval. The latter she had plenty of experience with before leaving London and all those who thought to judge her.

The statement she was greeted with was said with firmness and brooked no argument.

How could she tell someone that self-important, that large, there would never be a convenient time to speak with him? The fact he knew her godmother had taken her back. Sarah thought the woman a pillar of discretion. Someone Sarah could depend on when those in her own family had washed their hands of her. It would have been useless to feign ignorance of who this man was seeking. After years of being on her own, Sarah's past seemed to have caught up to her.

Sarah's godmother had warned her such a proposition might be offered. Since she had left society behind so long ago, she did not think the *ton's* memory so long or that anyone, any man, would go to such lengths to make her a sordid offer. After all, London was filled with the type of woman willing to sell her virtue to be seen on the arm of such a man. Especially if that man also had the wealth to dress in that manner and have such fine horses.

Her first instinct was to send him on his way. Only the thought he had gotten his information from Lady Winters had Sarah swallowing the harsh rebuke that first entered her mind. Perhaps her godmother thought this a good idea. A possibility of redemption.

His first words had stopped her midstride. Sarah had convinced herself the world she had once known, the people she had grown-up with and missed even after all this time, were lost to her. Not that she would have done anything differently if she had known the outcome, but this man's words woke a deep longing for what once had been her life. She had known the possibility of becoming an outcast when she committed herself to her fiancé. The problem was that no one had known of their secret relationship. Christopher had been due to go to the Peninsular and fight alongside other men wearing the bright red coats of a soldier. They had kept their betrothal secret since both families would have been against their marrying after such a brief period of knowing one another.

Sarah had promised her parents she would use her first season to learn how to go on before forming any attachments. Her parents wished her to have at least a second season before selecting a mate for life, and she had agreed to that—in the beginning. Little did she know she would meet the man of her dreams a few days after arriving in London.

Although they noticed her preference for the young lieutenant, her family thought she needed to meet more potential mates before choosing a marriage partner. Men with titles and wealth were being considered by her parents as her future husband.

It had only been within weeks of the season beginning when she and Christopher decided they were in love. After meeting Christopher, nothing and no one else seemed to match up. No one made her feel the same way. He was everything any girl could have wished. He had blond hair and blue eyes and a grin that never missed to make her heart jump a little. The dimples on each side of his mouth were cherubic and tantalizing at the same time.

Her gazing at them was the last thing she remembered doing before their first kiss. And what a kiss. She felt as if she were floating all the way home in her parent's carriage that night. Afterward, Christopher and she had made sure to find a way to steal a kiss at every ball and rout where they found themselves together. As a newly enlisted man and grandson of an earl, he had entry everywhere in London. As an officer going off to fight England's enemies, he was sought out by most all the young debutants. Sarah felt a need to tie him to her, to keep his attention on her. To prevent him from wandering and possibly forgetting about her while he was in Spain.

Well, her plans went awry as most plans do when not given time to formulate. Christopher was called up to leave on a ship to Portugal, and Sarah found herself with child and facing her deeply unhappy parents. Ways for the young couple to wed were quickly discussed between both sets of parents, but news of Christopher's death occurred without confirmation he could have fathered the child and his family turned their backs to her.

Their chilling, accusing eyes would forever brand her. It was as if she had brought about the death of their son instead of offering them a part of him that still lived. The whole *ton* turned their back on her since it had been decided there was no proof who the father was, and therefore, she was left shunned and shamed. Her father gave her money, part of the money he said he would have made as a dowry, and washed his hands of her. She remembered the red rimmed eyes of her mother as Sarah was driven away in a hired carriage without a destination or a friend in the world.

The interloping man had stared straight at her expecting some sort of response. She could come up with none. Did she wish to become respectable again? Here in Little Castleton, she was respected even though everyone knew she had birthed a child out of wedlock. And when that same child was said to have died, they still allowed her to stay and become one of them.

Sarah knew she had been breathing hard, trying to prevent the conversation from exploding into a denial of everything he was saying. There had been an attraction between them, Christopher and her, as soon as they met. It grew into so much more, and yet everyone said they could not be together. There did not seem to be enough time, and they were so desperate. Christopher had given her a ring, and they knew they were betrothed even if everyone else thought differently. They were so in love...

Tears flooded her eyes just as they did whenever she thought about that time and their tender emotions for one another. So strong she could feel the ache of him leaving for the ship even yet. The grief she felt when she read his death notice in the *Times* printed along with all the others who had perished in the battle alongside him. She had taken some comfort in the fact he had not been alone. That he had been with friends in his last moments. She had recognized several of the other names in the article as belonging to young men she had danced with.

That portion of her life was over. She had an opportunity to salvage something of her life. Salvage something of the life Topher would have had if she and her lieutenant had married as he expected. The viscount had made her a proposition that could not be denied outright. Might not be denied at all.

He was honest about his reasons for marriage. He was honest about his love of another woman. He was honest about everything as far as Sarah could tell.

Each person has certain endeavors in their life they feel they need to meet by certain ages. Perhaps he thought he would have been married by now. Sarah began to understand the viscount's marriage proposal.

Biting her lip, she realized he was the only person who understood what she had tried to do when she first found she was with child. Lessen Christopher's parent's loss by offering his child in his place. The fact it was a boy should have helped them in their grief, but they refused to even admit the possibility that Christopher and she had been betrothed or that their son could have left a child behind. Admittedly a child he had not known about, but still a part of him. Part of Christopher and her. She had never thought about abandoning the infant to another family to raise as their own. That won this man a point, but she did not know if it was enough.

CHAPTER TWO

Riding back in the enclosed carriage, Tony pulled the greatcoat closer to his body. This damp fall English air felt too cool to his skin after years on the Continent and more recently, Italy. Even after the uncertainty of his plan, he was quite proud of himself. Not only had he found the young woman he had begun seeking only a fortnight ago, he had completed the tricky negotiations to accomplish what he wished. When Marguerite had brought up the idea of his finding a biddable wife to give him the heir he needed, he had doubted a young woman of proper birth could be found to accept such an offer. After all, most women married to gain access to society and a title, not hide away from it.

When his mother mentioned the sad fact of Miss Jamieson's life, she had not been doing so to encourage his interest, he was sure. She had merely been stating that her friend thought her goddaughter had been caught in a difficult position from which neither family wished to help her escape. After all, if this Lieutenant Geoffrey had lived, he certainly would have married the young woman as soon as he was able, and the families would have stood firm in their acceptance of such an occurrence. Especially given the circumstances of war interrupting what otherwise would have been an acceptable marriage.

Instead, her misfortune became leverage in which to talk her into accepting his less than welcomed offer. If the child had lived, he would have added his support of the boy in getting into the right schools and meeting the right people, but that was not how life had dealt with the young woman. So, along with her reputation, she had lost both the father of the child and child within months of one another. Tragic, but perhaps his offer would be construed in the manner he had made it. He wished something from her and was not averse to offering something of value in return. Being able to show up on a London street without being shunned should be enough—for now. In the future, after providing him the heirs and any other children they should be blessed with, she could enter society as his wife. By then he and Marguerite would probably be back in Italy where they would be living the life they had been used to living.

It was strange how quickly he had forgotten the staid and proper London rules. How and when men and women should interact or in many cases ignore one another. Admittedly the Continental approach to marriage and mistresses was much more liberal than England's. He did not think his relationship with his *contessa* would have flourished as it had if they had met in England. Even a strong association with a widow was not acceptable to a man who needed to marry to secure the title, let alone under his parent's eyes. They would not have been as open and social as they were able to be while traveling or living in Italy where Marguerite had continued to maintain a household after her husband's death.

Marguerite—her beauty still took his breath away even after all these years. Dark flashing eyes and ebony hair, creamy skin bearing the kiss of the sun which was inescapable in the hot region of the Mediterranean. She loved the seaside, and he loved making her happy. They had been the couple everyone wished to invite to their homes and villas. It was a never-ending party going from one visitation to another while barely stepping foot in the villa he rented in the seaside town they made their port of call.

Pulling his greatcoat up round his neck to prevent the cool air from winding its way inside, he thought of this new life. He returned home to see to his estate and to make sure his mother was being taken care of. He found her living with her widowed sister, both women comfortably off and happy to be independent enough to decide where they went and who they saw. Neither attended evening events often and kept to visiting their older friends still living in London during the afternoons. It was one more worry off his mind since his mother and Marguerite would never meet that he could see. Neither was awake when the other was.

But his mother, and aunt for that matter, made it plain his duty lay in procuring a young wife and getting her with child. He had reluctantly agreed in principle, and Marguerite's suggestion sealed the prospect. He would marry a woman who knowingly would allow him to continue to live as he wished while providing him with the children everyone seemed to think he needed. He was not averse to doing so and was pleased when he heard about Miss Jamieson and her possibly agreeing to his plan. A woman who seemed to prefer the country life. One willing to trade her village life to one in a manor house.

He was also pleased she was as attractive as her godmother had implied. From what he, saw of her, other than her manner of dress, she was a lady. She had not whimpered or tried to hide the fact she had a child out of wedlock even if she could have since the child had not lived long enough for anyone to know of its existence. Her chestnut-colored hair had been half hidden behind a plain mob-cap, but her hazel eyes were arresting, appearing greener in moments of intense emotion. Her intelligence was evident in her quick thinking and ability to live hidden so well while living out in the open at the same time.

Her hazel eyes had pooled with tears, but only those of grief and loss, never for her own plight. Perhaps it was because she did not blame anyone for her circumstance. She could have secretly gone off to visit friends in the country and left the child with some farmer and his wife who already had too many children to care for. Forgotten all about the child and his dead father, but she had not, and he thought highly of the courage that must have taken at the time. Especially since her godmother had also had a few choice words for the young man's family and their dismissal of their own grandchild simply because the couple had not had time to marry before their son had been shipped out. The bad luck of his dying during the first battle he engaged in was also unforeseen in a long line of bad timing and happenstance.

Perhaps it had been a cheap-shot saying anything about the poor quality of her dress and living, but he did not have much besides his money and title on offer. Certainly not love or fondness, not even his fidelity which he was already stretching even if Marguerite agreed with the need for him to take a wife.

Shaking his head, he wished to keep the two women separate even in his thoughts. It would be the only way he could continue with the plan. Agree to tie his life and family to a woman he had never met, but who would be desperate enough to agree to his offer. While at the same time keeping the woman he had pledged to love till his dying day. A woman who had spent years by his side teaching him the ways of the world and the ways of love. He owed his allegiance to Marguerite, and his wife would need to understand where his loyalty lay.

But he had not been prepared to meet such a woman as Miss Jamieson. He was not sure what he expected, but not the self-contained, independent young woman he found working like a servant in a garden reading it for the winter. It appeared as if she lived alone, as well. The investigator had not mentioned anyone else living in the house. The red-vested man had mentioned Miss Jamieson was supporting herself making and selling lace, but nothing of any friends or visitors.

The report held fairly little about the woman herself although that had not been the job the Bow Street Runner was to perform. He was to find the young lady, and Tony would do the rest. The man probably thought Tony wished to offer the woman *carte blanche* and not the legitimate proposal he made. If such an offer could be considered legitimate. Although to be honest, it was not much different than many *ton* marriages turned out to be. The only thing was that Tony was being honest up front and making sure his wife would be agreeable to his terms.

Miss Jamieson seemed to have been. She was not shocked but seemed to take his words to heart. He could see she was thinking over how the life would affect her and his admiration for her increased with every question she asked and with her thoughtful consideration. He had not had to point out the benefits; she could see them for herself. The only thing holding her back was whether or not to give up her independence, he could tell. Wondering if she could believe that his offer was all he said it was.

If need be, when he returned, he would offer more freedom after the first male child was born. Possibly she, too, could look forward to a life with love and companionship. Perhaps he would send her a letter stating the benefits one more time to ensure she did not back-out and decide to take her chances that time alone would win her way back into society.

****

What had she done? What had she agreed to? Was the proposition as good as she first thought, or had she possibly put herself and all those she loved in jeopardy? Was the man as blasé about her history, about her bearing a child without benefit of marriage and then insisting upon keeping that child? Making all the arrangements to live in the country, forsaking all those who told her to rid herself of the child or face censure. Face the shunning of her friends and peers.

Walking briskly on the trail which cut across fields and over fences, she thought about the prospect of becoming some man's wife. A woman who would bear him children, but not have anything else to do with his life. Run the home she lived in and raise the children in the manner acceptable to the viscount. It sounded almost too good to be true, but she believed him when he said he loved his widow, and Sarah could understand how this agreement would alleviate his problems. Allow him to continue as he had always done with the widow and have a legal, competent wife who would give him his freedom to do as he wished without censure or fuss. She could be that wife as far as not caring what the man did. She had already decided she would never marry or have more children. The fact he also had enough money to make being married while having another household or two to care for was a benefit. A benefit she could take advantage of and put her plans in action as well as have what she wished out of life. The life she thought she would be denied once she read that Christopher had been killed in battle.

Of course, there would always be those who stood by her even if from a distance, such as her godmother. She had received a few notes from the lady telling Sarah of her mother's health which was declining and her father's irritability which was not. It would not help Sarah if she lost the few people who had stood by her and her unpopular decision.

And things had changed for her. Medical costs surrounding Topher's birth and first few months had taken much of the ready cash she had, and she was now supplementing where she could. Lace making which had begun as a calming hobby now became a source of income even though selling it in Greater Castleton was not as profitable as selling it in a larger city such as London, but she was never going to return to London.

Lord Wyndom had been correct in thinking she cared very little for anything or anyone living there. Only her mother, who was now more or less confined to the upstairs rooms of the family townhouse. It pained Sarah to think about the woman unable to even make it down a set of steps on her own, her arthritis being so bad in knees and hips.

So much seemed to have changed in the two years she had been gone from London. The two years where she hid who and what she was only to be found by a man seeking an undemanding wife. A wife who would be glad to be married under any circumstance even to a man who admitted, no boasted, he would never care anything for her. Who would never feel anything for her other than perhaps gratitude for getting with child quickly and then producing, in quick order, two heirs.

She did not doubt she could become pregnant very quickly considering it had only taken one time with Christopher. The night before he was to leave...their passion overwhelmed them as they talked about his leaving and perhaps not returning for years. They were able to sneak away to the back of the garden and make love. It was not exactly as she imagined it would be, but then what ever is? She did not have anyone to ask any questions of, and Christopher was almost as inexperienced as she. She did not ask, but he seemed to know somewhat what to do while she tried to follow his lead and understand her part. No matter how it occurred, she became with child. She had immediately sent a letter through the army mail but was not sure if Cristopher ever received the news. In a way she hoped he had, and that he had been glad. Glad that he had something to live for and come home to besides Sarah. A reason to make it back to both of them.

Wiping a tear from her eye, she refused to allow herself to feel sorry for anything that happened. It was as it was, and no amount of rethinking anything would alter that. She needed to decide if she could live with this new choice if she accepted the viscount's offer.

Climbing over the last stile, she inhaled the cool air deeply hoping to clear her mind to focus on the most important matter. Remembering how she became pregnant might be the biggest stumbling block. Could she be intimate with a stranger no matter what it brought her in benefits and moved her forward in her plans? Make those plans complete before they could even be implemented?

Could she allow another man access to her most intimate parts and allow that man to leave his seed within her? Making love with Christopher had been the most intimate thing she had ever done with anyone. A passionate kiss, again with Christopher, came in a close second, but Christopher was much closer to her age and had about as much experience.

Thinking about the size of the man who had stood in her garden arguing the pros of becoming his wife and giving him legitimate heirs was so much more. He was not only older in years but had been having an affair with a widow for eight years and who knows what with other women before that. She thought he must have had some experience prior to his widow.

Not that she was trying to compete or win his ardor, but she did not wish them to laugh over her inexperience—her gaucheness. It did not seem like something that should happen. Perhaps she could write it into the contract. That intimate matters would remain between the two parties participating. She certainly did not wish to know what he was doing with his widow, either.

Now that left only the part she had been circling, but not addressing. Could she actually have a stranger enter her body? Allow Lord Wyndom the access he needed to beget children and no more. No other touching or fondling or…anything. How would one write that into a contract? No, it would have to be something they agreed upon and hopefully never have to discuss it again. She hoped she could broach the subject, for if she could not before they were married, then it would be too late afterwards if he did not agree.

Approaching the larger village of Greater Castleton, she walked directly to the small shop next to the tavern and inn. The slanted roof always reminded her of a house about to collapse onto itself, but she knew the building, like the town, had been there for over two hundred years perhaps longer, but rebuilt after a fire wiped out most of the buildings.

"Missus Smith, I wuz just speakin' of ya. I could use more of your lace for Missus Ferguson's collar. She wishes a new winter frock, and the squire told her to spare no costs so handmade lace it is."

The seamstress who ran the small shop met Sarah with the information as soon as the door opened. She was a corpulent woman who looked as if sewing anything stylish was so far from her ability as to be ludicrous, but it only went to show how appearances could be deceiving. The woman was as fine a modiste as any found on Bond Street.

"If you need more, I can make the same pattern, Mrs. Tanner. Or if you wish it out of heavier thread, that is always an option as well. It would hold up to more washings that way."

"No, what ye bring me is right fine. She saw it already, and it's been approved. You off to Lucy's as usual?" At Sarah's nod the woman continued, "Tell her ma hello from me, and that I got that yarn in she's been waitin' on."

"Oh, I can take it for her."

"No, none of that now. If she don't have a reason to

come and see me, how am I to do any gossipin'?" She cackled showing the missing teeth on the side of her mouth.

Smiling, Sarah responded, "I shall tell her, but take the costs out of my proceeds. I feel she does most of her knitting for me."

Sarah left the store with a few more coins than she came in with and headed to the end of the lane leading out of town to the north.

*****

Sarah saw Lucy open the door after looking out the front window. Sarah hurried forward bending down to scoop up the small child trying to stand on his own, but wavering in his happiness to see her coming toward him.

"How is my big boy? Mm-m-m-m, I missed you so much." She left the sound of a big smack from her lips hanging in the air as she lifted the baby into her arms and carried him back into the heated cottage.

He placed his chubby arms around her neck saying, "My momma. Mine."

"Yes, I am and proud of it, my little one."

"He's been asking about you more and more lately. Maybe we should rethink what we have planned," Lucy said, glancing as if for support toward the older woman sitting near the hearth.

Sarah interrupted the others' words. "That seems serendipitous since I have come to speak about a new plan that shall make things much easier for all of us."

The three women sat down at the table after placing a piece of crust in the baby's hands.

The two others looked so much alike even though there was a generation separating them, Sarah had to keep from commenting upon it again. Lucy's mother was in her late forties and had a passel of children born and raised. All, but Lucy gone and living in their own homes.

Lucy, blue eyed and blonde haired was a younger version of her mother, but with a little more life to her motions. Of course, being barely over twenty, the younger woman had not been beaten down by life. Or by the hard work and worry it took to raise a family, even though Lucy was making things easier for her mother by living at home and contributing to the costs with the money Sarah paid her for caring for Topher Jeffery.

The two watched Sarah expectantly since this was not something they had planned.

"I have been offered a chance to marry a man my godmother in London knows." A stretch of the truth, but she did not wish her friends to worry she did not know what she was doing or that the man in question was not safe to wed.

Both women inhaled before beginning to ask questions and putting their worries into words. "But Sarah," Lucy began just as her mother said, "Who would do such a thing?"

Blushing, the older woman explained, "Not that I don't think it a good thing, but who do you know who you would marry in Little Castleton—or even here for that matter?"

The woman had a small view of life, and those two villages made up her world. She knew about London and worried the whole time Lucy had been employed as a lady's maid there working for Sarah's father. Lucy left with Sarah when Sarah's father threw Sarah from their home. The moral support and Lucy's knowledge of how to get on in the world saved Sarah from more hurt and harm then she could ever repay.

"I understand your surprise, Mrs. Coop, but he is the son of a good friend of my godmother. He is Lady Wyndom's son and newly made viscount."

"Oh, I remember her." Lucy had a wide smile as if remembering the woman and liking what she remembered. "You met her in the park one day while walking. She was with your godmother in a grand carriage, and they pulled to the side to speak with you."

"You are correct, Lucy, and I ran into her at several functions during the first weeks of the season…before I met Christopher." As if saying the man's name brought her thoughts back to her son, she placed her hand on his head as he drooled messily down the apron covered dress he wore. "We spoke, but only the barest of conversations asking about one's health or speaking of the weather. I do not think she knows he has approached me."

"Approached you? As in what do you mean, Lady Sarah? Did he make you an improper offer?" Mrs. Coop was staring right at her as if she could see if the man had said anything untoward.

"No, it was a forthright proposal—with a few conditions." Now the difficult part came as to how much to tell these two women who had gone out of their way to help a young woman with an illegitimate baby in her belly and no one else to give her aid. "Viscount Wyndom does not really wish a wife but feels he must secure the title with an heir. Since I have proven myself fertile, his words not mine, he thought I would be grateful for his name. There have been two new seasons since I came out. After all, no one else is going to offer for me. I am sure no one even remembers me any longer, but if I showed my face in London, they would remember soon enough."

"There is much about you, Lady Sarah, that speaks well and perhaps his mother reminded him of that when he was looking for a bride," Lucy's mother said nodding.

Lucy seemed to be more aware of how the world worked, at least, the world in London. "Why did he ask you, Sarah, and none of what sounds good versus what he really said."

Leave it to Lucy to get to the brass tacks of things. "He has a mistress that he refuses to give up. In fact, he would marry her, but she is older and cannot have children so they have decided it best for him to marry a woman who would be happy to settle anywhere besides London. He thought that sounded like me plus I have had a child so am proven fertile."

"Oh, my," Mrs. Coop said, appearing worried, but not saying anything more leaving it to Lucy to get to the bottom of things.

"What do you think, Sarah? I know you've been worrying over this since he spoke with you. And when exactly was that?"

Grimacing, Sarah said, "Yesterday afternoon. He made a good point for doing it. Marrying him, I mean. As a married woman, I could possibly enter society again. At least visit my mother and godmother openly. He assured me I would be very well maintained in his country home and have funds to do with as I wish."

Both women's brows rose almost to their hairline, but it was Mrs. Coop who spoke. "Well, that's a whole different story then is it not, my lady. What with those funds, taking care of Master Topher here would be much easier. Make a way for him to get into a proper school when the time comes, too, I bet."

"Yes, and he shall have possible siblings to play

with until that time comes, as well."

Now it was time for Lucy to rub the small boy's hair as he gnawed on the chair's rung. "We knew it was going to happen eventually and perhaps this is the best time after all. My man has asked me to marry him, and I've said yes. I think I may already be with child, so it is not a matter of if, but of when." They all laughed at her joke.

Sarah looked at her friend and her heart rose then sank. "I am so glad for you, but I had hoped to take you with me to Wyngate, wherever that is. I am sure I can find a job for Toby as long as he doesn't have his heart set on a particular one."

"No, just something more permanent than what he's been doing around here. He's a hard worker and knows about doing most anything around a farm or estate. Maybe not inside like a footman, but anything else," she told Sarah honestly, and it was not anything Sarah had not already thought about. Toby was a solid mass of manpower, but not someone you wished around precious vases or gewgaws.

"Well, I have been told I shall have the ability to change anyone and hire whomever I wish, so I think I can find a place once we get there." Sarah looked at the two women who had stayed by her side all through these past two years. Lucy, who had been her lady's maid and Mrs. Coop, who had been her original nursemaid before leaving to raise her own family when Sarah grew old enough. The older woman later sent Lucy into service with Sarah's family when she reached an age. Now they were trusting in Sarah one more time and tying their future to hers. She hoped she was not making a mistake by accepting Lord Wyndom's offer, but what else was there for her? Working her way back into society would be difficult enough. Towing a bastard child would make such a move impossible, and this plan of Lord Wyndom gave Topher the best chance of getting into a school and possibly being accepted in society in some manner.

She could not force the boy's grandparents to accept him, but anyone who knew Lieutenant Christopher Geoffrey could see the boy was his spitting image. There would be no doubt who fathered the boy she bore, but she had decided long ago they did not deserve to see Christopher's son after being so disparaging when they first learned of his existence.

But could she raise her son and be a good wife and mother to Lord Wyndom's heir? She knew she would love any children she bore, but that would mean accepting their father into her bed, into her body. That was the most pressing issue before her. That and the fact Topher would need to be kept in the background. He would never be accepted completely into society with the taint of not having his father's last name, never knowing his father or his father's family. All because of the mistiming of his parents being intimate.

Sarah needed to think, but right now she wished to enjoy her time with her son. She had little enough of it with him as it was. Bending, she picked him up from the floor to cuddle him.

"All right, my big boy. What should we do today?"

After spending all the time she could with Topher, Sarah walked home while her mind returned to her original worry. Lord Wyndom and whether she could be his wife and bear his children and ignore society's gossiping about him and his mistress.

Deciding society did not matter to her one way or the other, she was satisfied it would not be an issue. After all, she had been through that gauntlet and come out without too much blood drawn. She had not been in the *ton's* vision for so very long before she met and fell in love with the dashing Lieutenant Geoffrey.

Sarah's mother insisted that first season was needed to position Sarah so she would secure a good husband. Her father had finally managed financially to do so as Sarah turned nineteen. A little older than most, but not so long in the tooth as to appear desperate.

She and her mother had poured over the pattern plates and materials selecting the best they could afford and adding the lace Sarah made herself. With additional fichus, ribbons, and shawls Sarah made her limited wardrobe seem much larger. A bonnet that she changed to match her dress made it seem she had more than the two, and her striped spencer went with multiple walking dresses. Sarah never felt at a disadvantage and was confident no one had discovered her secret of changing out trimmings to fashion a new ballgown. That is where Lucy became indispensable. Her maid's small quick stitches could re-make an entire dress in an afternoon. The girl's ability to visualize a finished product while constructing it made her a genius.

Sarah entered society on the arm of her father and then was off on her own. It had been exciting and exhilarating and exhausting, but she had loved it. Seeing London and doing the inexpensive things like visiting the museums and a few of the subscription balls were enough for Sarah. Her godmother had gotten her invitations to a few of the *ton's* more exclusive homes where the beauty of the architecture and paintings and other art on display was enchanting. It was at one of these homes she met Lieutenant Geoffrey in his resplendent uniform. He asked her to dance for the first time and then spent the supper dance sitting next to her plying her with goodies from the laden table.

It did not take long before Sarah was searching the room for the lieutenant each time she arrived anywhere. Soon, she was telling him her itinerary, and she would find the young man there ahead of her. It was a wonderful, wonderful time in her life.

Then the letter came that Christopher was to be shipped out without much notice. Sooner than he had thought, but spring must come earlier in Spain than England and battles were being fought. Men were needed to boost the number going against the enemy, and men were being called away. Young men with so much living left to do.

Her mind shied away from those few days when they knew he was leaving and her inability to do anything about it. She tried but failed to convince her family she was old enough to know her own mind and be allowed to accept Christopher's proposal. They told her she would have time later to do so. That she had barely been in London to see or meet very many young men and that she had promised to wait until the season was over before forming an attachment.

But those promises had been made before she had met Christopher. Before their love bloomed, and she realized love did not follow a timeline. It was not something you planned for or that waited until one was ready. That was when her heart broke, and she wished she could go with Christopher instead of having to remain at home worrying about him.

Now she was making a life decision based on her mind and not her heart. It was easier to do, she found.

She knew what would be best for Topher, and he was all that mattered. He had her heart and always would, so making this decision was not as difficult as she at first thought. Allowing Lord Wyndom access to her body really would not matter. Something to get through and then he would be gone and her lovely child would have a life Sarah never thought possible for him, for them.

She would do this. She would be a stranger's wife, mother to his children, and Topher would have a viscountess as a mother and admission to anywhere Sarah thought best for him. Proper tutors and prep school. Possibly university and entry to school friends' homes and access to their families. He would be a part of the life he was meant to have.

CHAPTER THREE

Sarah jostled the basket sitting on the leather seat next to her. She glanced over to the older lady accompanying her to see how she fared being tossed about due to the rutted roads they were traversing. It was difficult to tell. Not that the woman was dour exactly, but she showed little emotion, not even smiling when she introduced herself as Mrs. Wilson, that morning. The meeting was brief since she had been expected. Expected to be the proper chaperone to stay with Sarah the time before her wedding which would be celebrated tomorrow morning.

The thought made a shiver go through Sarah. She had met her future husband two times for less than an hour total. The man was concise and certain. She had to admire him for that. A viscount who could get things done. She had the feeling he used very little help to get the wedding license, the church and clergy arranged, and this carriage which was taking her to an inn outside of London so she would have a short trip tomorrow to the church.

And, of course, Mrs. Wilson dressed in widow's black appearing formidable rather than the kind one took pity on. For some reason, Sarah thought the woman had possession of a weapon upon her person, perhaps a small pocket pistol of some sort. The kind ladies sometimes carried when attending gaming hells without their guardians' knowledge.

Unsure how Sarah felt about the weapon, and the woman's one-word answers to any questions she had asked so far, Sarah kept her questions and thoughts to herself. She also hoped this woman disappeared once they were at the church in the morning. Sarah did not relish this woman as a witness to her wedding.

Her wedding. How could she honestly say she had any ownership of the ceremony that would tie her to a man she barely knew and for reasons she would not admit to anyone besides a priest in a confessional? She knew nothing of the church, the man who would officiate, or where they would go after those momentous words had been spoken.

She would become that man's possession in the eyes of the world, the law and even her God. Clenching her fingers together, she hoped the woman across from her had not noticed the trembling. Sarah was sure the woman was a spy for the viscount as well as her guard. What would happen if she ordered the carriage to stop? Stop right there and let her descend to the road beneath them and walk away?

But where would she walk? How would she get away from the promises she had already made even if they had not been in front of a cleric of the church? Would Mrs. Wilson take measures to stop her? To follow her? Pull that little gun Sarah was sure the older woman carried from her reticule?

Closing her eyes to prevent the other woman from seeing the turmoil going through her mind, Sarah focused on how serious a predicament she was in. How dangerous it would be for all concerned if she had misjudged the man she agreed to marry. Not simply marry, but provide an heir to. A man who she had spoken to for less than an hour.

Any man could be suave and polite for an hour, could he not? Any man could look the part of a gentleman for an hour, but what if he wasn't. What if he was not what he pretended to be just as she was doing? Perhaps that was what was eating at her all this time. That she was perpetrating a falsehood upon him so why would she assume he was not doing the same? Was it only her guilt that was making her uneasy?

Glancing over to the other woman, she saw she was dosing to the rhythm of the hoof beats of the four horses pulling them and the now more constant swaying of the carriage. Plus, the woman had probably been in the carriage at least an hour before picking Sarah up in Little Castleton where she had finished packing what was left of her personal belongings. Lucy, Mrs. Coop, and Topher were already travelling to the viscount's estate and would be established by the time she arrived.

Toby had been assured a job. That had been part of the agreement or rather, as the viscount preferred to call it, their marriage contract. He had dealt with her as he would have her father if the man had wished to be a part of things. Sarah insisted she handle all such paperwork, and Lord Wyndom had offered the use of a solicitor from the legal associates he used in London. Sarah declined not wishing any more people being aware of what was going on than necessary. It was not called a sale, but that was what it was. She was selling herself, her body for that man's personal and intimate use…and for what in return?

They thought it was for propriety. So, she would be received in London parlors for tea or social functions, to dance and parade her fine clothes and hair in front of others doing the same. Exchanging wickedly cruel comments about others younger or prettier than she was. As she stood among the dowers and women thought to be too old to dance and therefore ignored. No, she was not doing this for those things and never would.

This marriage, this sale of herself was to one day be able to introduce her son into the society he should have always been a part of. Topher would never be or have what he should have, but with the education and clothes and access to travel this marriage would allow her to shower on him, he would come close. It would help if his paternal grandparents acknowledged him, but if they never did, it would be their loss. Their lost chance to have a bit of their son back.

Inhaling deeply, she turned her mind to what this marriage would bring her that she cared about. The money was first and foremost. The marriage settlements were all in her favor as she did not have funds to speak of any longer. The viscount had set a sum aside for her dower portion saying he hoped she would not have need of them for a very long time. His lips did not curve up at all, so Sarah had a difficult time knowing whether he was teasing or merely being practical. He seemed the pragmatic kind of man.

Then there was her monthly stipend which was more than generous considering it was accompanied by a clothing allowance which he informed her would be increased if she found she needed more, a carriage and driver at her disposal, trips to town after the birth of the first son and use of the family jewels or at least the ones his mother did not need while she was in society. Much more than she should expect. Much more than she would have had if she had followed the drum and married Christopher.

The carriage slowed, and they drew to a stop inside the walls of the courtyard to a small inn. Mrs. Wilson roused herself and peered around getting her bearings as the sound of the step being lowered brought Sarah's attention to the door.

"A brief stop to rest and dine, my lady. I shall come for you when the horses have been watered and rested as well," the middle-aged groomsman told her.

"Thank you. Mrs. Wilson and I would appreciate the break and I assume a cup of tea?" She turned toward the older lady who nodded and waited for Sarah to leave the carriage first.

*****

Sarah stared hard into the mirror trying to see the young woman she had been a mere two years ago. So much had happened, and that was a prelude to what she had committed herself to from now on. From this day forward, not only would this man, this stranger be in charge of her life, he would by being her husband be in charge of Topher's, as well, even if he never found out about the boy.

But at some point, it would be inevitable. Topher would be with her at a moment where their relationship would be evident. Her husband would hear of her spending too much time with the child or find an incriminating receipt for the boy's school costs or question her closeness to her maid's family, especially the woman's eldest son.

And would her plans to keep Topher with Mrs. Coop be possible? The woman was getting older, and originally Lucy was to care for him, but now... She could allow Lucy to stay at home and pay her from Sarah's own stipend. Perhaps that would be the best way since Lucy was with child as well. Mrs. Coop would never be able to watch two young children. Not at her age or with her bad knees.

"It's time, my lady." The longest sentence Mrs. Wilson had spoken since she had arrived to pick Sarah up from her cottage yesterday morning.

In a couple of hours, Sarah would become Viscountess Wyndom and have all the privileges that title gave her. Everything she had meant to achieve when she accepted her first invitation to dance at her first cotillion. Her parents would have been so pleased, but that pleasure was not to be shared. If they learned of her rise in prestige, would they soften and forgive her other transgression? Could they?

Possibly, but they would never accept her son. The proof they failed to instill proper beliefs and maidenly virtue into her. They had washed their hands of her, and she of them even if it still hurt to think of them. Of what they were missing not knowing their grandson.

The streets were much better the closer to town they drove. Sarah prevented herself from craning her neck out of the window to catch the city waking-up. The pink rays of sunrise cast a lovely glow as a backdrop to the buildings as they drove into the now bustling streets and then the still quiet business district. She knew these streets would be teeming by noontime, but the sights and sounds of London left her cold.

Peering out the window now they were stopping, she saw flower vendors setting up their impermanent stalls along with the women holding baskets of nosegays and stemmed flowers available to those attending the ceremonies which occurred daily at the church's chapels.

Sarah prepared to step out when Mrs. Wilson's hand descended on her arm. The first time the woman touched her without the need to help Sarah dress.

"My lady, do not think too harshly of him. He is a good man and shall do as he promises. Do not fear he is not what he seems."

The seriousness in the older woman's eyes and her earnest words had Sarah nodding in understanding. The woman did not wish to become too involved in what was to occur today, but did trust the man involved. Sarah must not have done as good a job at hiding her own fears as she thought. She tried to smile but felt her face frozen so simply nodded as she stepped out.

She was surprised to hear her carriage pull away and looked back at the retreating equipage. Evidently, just as Sarah felt she could bond with the older woman, it was to find that woman whisked away probably never to be seen again.

Turning toward a man approaching her, she accepted his bow. "My lady, I am Brian Lloyd, Esquire, at your service. I am to give you this bouquet and walk you to the chapel."

Startled from her reverie began by her chaperone's words, Sarah hoped she smiled and accepted the fragrant flowers from the man dressed impressively for an attorney. She accepted his arm and began walking toward the door to the imposing St. George Cathedral albeit a less grand door than most attendees used. This was probably into a smaller side chapel where she would be married.

It may have been a lesser chapel, but no less breathtaking and overwhelming in its grandeur. The altar was gilded and candles glowed shimmering up the stone walls and an impressive number of pews and seats lining the long aisle leading to the priest and viscount standing in the multi-hued light streaming through the stained-glass window.

Somewhere along the way, the attorney had removed his curled brimmed top hat and was now leading her toward the two men. Her legs trembled, but she forced herself to continue on this path. On the path to financial freedom for her and all those who she loved and cared about. The path to future possibilities that would benefit all of them. The path that would tie her life to this stranger's for as long as she lived.

She tried to focus on the crucifix above the men and hoped she was not seeing her future in the expression of despair in the face of the Christ on the cross. Was this a forewarning? Was this a sign she should not take these vows, commit herself to this man? Commit her son to this man even if the viscount did not know of Topher's existence?

The words Mrs. Wilson said to her before they parted returned. Sarah did trust the man she was walking toward. She did think he was good and honest and was entering this marriage for all the reasons he had told her. She would accept her fate and learn to live with a man who she knew loved another and would spend his time with that other woman. No deceptions needed. No recriminations or blame or guilt for either of them.

She felt the first real smile cross her face as she dropped the attorney's arm and accepted the viscounts in its place. They turned toward the priest as the solicitor moved to stand to the side of her husband-to-be. The priest's words were heard but were not the focus of her thoughts.

Instead, she was noting how much taller and larger the man to her side was or at least felt to her now. He had always been wearing that many-caped greatcoat and hat so she had been misjudging the size of the man himself. Wearing a dark morning coat with tails, white shirt covered with a light blue waistcoat and laced edged cravat bearing a darker blue stone pin holding it in place, he was impressive. His legs appeared long and strong, and she tried to concentrate on the priest's words rather than the strikingly handsome man beside her. A man who would own her body and soul after she uttered those vows the priest would put to her.

Well, perhaps not her soul. She would always be her own person no matter how many pledges she took. Too independent, her parents had said so many times before they accepted the fact, she would rather give up society, a good marriage, even them before she would give up the child she carried. The child that proved she had loved once so deeply she threw away all chances of a different life. The life they had planned for her. So instead, they turned their backs and allowed her to pack and leave taking only her lady's maid with her for support.

Shaking her head to clear her mind of past sorrows, she drew the attention of the man now holding her hand and slipping his ring onto it. A simple band which she thought appropriate for the wife left in the country to provide heirs. A simple band, but more than she should be expecting from any man. Any man, besides the father to her child. A man buried in some field in Spain who would never be able to give her that band. She had only his signet ring which she still wore on her right hand, middle finger.

She tried to smile and accept the token of this man's vows. His loyalty and care which she knew he would never have offered her if he had not been in need of a woman who he thought would accept the less than appealing offer. The offer to remain hidden away in the country. At least for the years of her youth producing his children until an ample number had been born at which time, she would have some freedom to perhaps find happiness.

It did not matter. None of it mattered if she could furnish Topher with a proper education at a school befitting a grandson of a baron and the great-grandson of an earl. Perhaps those links to the *ton* would be enough. Enough to allow him to enter society and pursue a woman who would not care that his parents had never wed. A woman who would love him and give him the family he deserved.

Sarah must remember her own selfish reasons for this marriage. She was not so pure as to blame anything on her more than generous husband. For that was who he was. According to the priest's last words. She was a married woman. Not to the man she assumed she would wed, but she was a married woman and as such had already gained the approval of many in society.

There was no chaste kiss between them, but he held her arm to guide her toward an open book on a rostrum with a quill and ink to the side. The viscount signed and then handed her the quill to do the same. The last time she would sign her maiden name. From now on she was someone else, and as such she planned on living an entirely different life.

Another set of papers were pushed in front of her. Looking up she met the gaze of the attorney, and he nodded toward the papers. "These are the final agreements that set out everything that was discussed between you. The marriage settlements and such…" He dipped the quill and handed it to her while her husband accepted congratulations from the clerics who must have been in the pews.

"Yes, certainly, Mr. Lloyd." Her eyes would not focus on all the words, but what she skimmed of them they were what she and the viscount had agreed to in the main. He was accepting her without a dowry and she was committing her body to him. Nothing unusual in that was there? The usual prize and price between man and wife.

They had forgone the need for any sort of celebratory meal since there were no guests present and climbed into a large coach pulled by four horses and accompanied by a driver, postillion and two footmen. The town was still in its waking period, before the roads out of town became busy while those heading into town were packed with all sorts of conveyances. The driver had no problem keeping the horses in check, but even Sarah could tell they wished to be out in the open spaces. She wondered how long before she reached the viscount's estate.

"My lord, I take it we shall make Wyngate prior to nightfall?"

He had been watching the throngs of people through the closed window but turned to her with a smile, as if making sure his mask was in place. "Yes, that is the plan, but we shall break our trip with a stop at a fine inn where they know me. We shall dine there and rest the horses and men before moving on."

Her stomach growled at the mention of possible food, and she pressed her hand into it while the man beside her chuckled. "Too nervous to eat this morning?"

Giving up the opportunity to pretend otherwise, she nodded. "I must confess I almost did not come to the church at all. If I thought I could order your driver to take me anywhere else I would have." Honesty was the only way she knew to go on if this agreement was to work. Her limited honesty at least. She felt he had been honest enough with her when he explained exactly what he needed from her.

"No, he probably would have delivered you to the church after all, but are you sorry he did so, now?" His blue eyes searched hers seeking the truth. As if her answer mattered to him.

"Not now. The ceremony was not as difficult as I thought, and I did not feel a complete fraud up there parroting those words. And your solicitor was very supportive." She glanced over his shoulder, unable to meet his gaze any longer. "I suppose I have you to thank for the lovely bouquet?" She glanced at the flowers on the other seat beginning to show the number of hours they had been out of water. "I shall dry them and make a potpourri for my clothing press."

"That sounds like a good use for them."

She was not sure if he was being facetious or not but decided to take the less egregious meaning and nodded before turning away from him and his searching eyes.

"Would you care to hear about the staff you shall be meeting this evening? I can go through the main ones since they were there prior to my leaving."

"When did you leave? I assume that was the last time you spent any time in England?"

"I left right after university. Actually, several of us went together, but the others made their way home within months of our tour. We all had expectations, and some were not met while others thought Europe and the various courts there accommodating and amusing."

"So, several young English men taking in all that the Continent has to offer? None of you had duties to fulfill?" She did not wish to think of Christopher right now, but he was close to the surface in her memory and she could not prevent herself.

"Most of us were the oldest son in the family so, no, entering service never crossed our minds, I am ashamed to say. One went back when his oldest brother died, and he was then heir apparent. Another went back to fulfill the promise to marry the young woman he was engaged to as soon as she had her first season. Four of us continued on for a few more months trying to ignore the fighting going on in Spain and the upheavals in France. It is surprising how much can be disregarded if there is enough liquor and entertainments to be had."

Knowing it was risky to tease without knowing his temperament, she took the chance. "For entertainments should I insert 'ladies' there?" She thought there was a slight flush to his cheeks, but she could not be sure since the light in the coach was not good.

"Of course, we were young men, and the better part of our time was used in searching for ladies who would flirt and spend time with us. It was innocent on both sides, and most were watched over by duennas or stern companions." His smile belied that statement, and she knew he had enjoyed more than light flirtations, but that probably had been with ladies of a different slant than ones who had duennas and chaperones to watch over their virtue.

To keep from the more personal questions she

asked, "Can you tell me about the cities you visited? Did you take any time to see the country itself that you were in or did you sleep all day and only rouse at night when the dancing and parties began?"

"We did some of both. We visited Brussels which was filled with escaping French aristocracy at the time. Not a happy place so we moved on to the German states and found them a little dark as well. St. Petersburg was bright and gay and filled with people trying to forget the possible Corsican's need to expand in that direction. It is a beautiful city right on the Gulf of Finland which opens to the Baltic Sea. And yes, it is as cold as you may have heard."

"Truly? The river freezes over and they skate on it?"

"The river freezes over and they drive sleighs on it. Build bonfires on the ice to keep those who venture out on it warm enough to remain outside. Alcohol and furs are what keep the people of St. Petersburg from freezing to death, I swear. I thought the use of furs was for effect, but soon found out differently and bought a fur lined coat and gloves."

His eyes were shining with memories. Good ones she thought, and he looked an entirely different man than the one she married only a few hours ago. He had several amusing stories about the people and places of St. Petersburg which she found she was very interested in hearing. Her world had been so small all her life.

The coach began to slow and turned into a courtyard where she could see hostlers standing waiting for their conveyance to come to a rocking halt.

"Luncheon, all ready?" she asked, not realizing how long they had been talking. How quickly the time flew past.

"I took the prerogative to preorder so we can be back on our way in a relatively short time. I booked a room for you to refresh yourself in and rest after our meal until we are ready to resume our trip." He helped her out of the coach while a footman went to the door to announce their arrival to the innkeeper.

The meal had been excellent, and Sarah was beginning to appreciate what a title could get you if one had one. The room she had been shown to had hot water as well as a young woman who offered to brush her skirt and cape. Sarah declined since she had not really walked anywhere to speak of and both were still clean. Instead, she took time to wash up and hurry downstairs hoping that would encourage the serving of the food which seemed to be ready. Perhaps the viscount had mentioned his wife was hungry to the innkeeper so the meal was presented as soon as Sarah arrived to the private room also set aside for their use.

"Were you able to rest?" he asked solicitously once they were both settled inside and the coach started off again.

"Yes, the excellent food and wine made me drowsy. In fact, I cannot guarantee not to fall asleep again as we travel. I am not used to such a substantial meal in the middle of the day."

His gaze moved over her body and returned to her eyes. "You need more such meals, if I may be allowed to say so. Probably more rest, too."

Teasing yet embarrassed by his personal comments, she asked, "Is that your way of saying I look tired and haggard, my lord?"

Taking her remark as she meant it, he smiled. "Not in the slightest, but I think you could use another stone to fill out some of the slender portions."

Feeling the blush move up from her neck to her cheeks, she looked out the window as if the fields dotted with sheep were the most intriguing things she had ever seen.

"Do not shut me out, Sarah. I merely wish you healthy and happy. It was not meant as a criticism."

Turning toward him, she said smiling, "I understand. To have a healthy heir you need a healthy mother. I remember what I am here for, my lord."

Blowing out air in one long breath, he said, "Perhaps you are more tired than you thought. Another rest might come in handy." Pulling her away from the cooler outside wall of the coach and onto his shoulder with one arm around her, she sat stiffly and uncomfortably against the man.

Eventually she relaxed and found him much more comfortable than she should and must have fallen asleep because she was woken when he removed his arm from around her slumped body. "Oh, I am sorry, my lord."

"It was fine. I must admit I took a cat nap as well. I was glad you trusted me enough to sleep." Straightening his sleeves, he reached for his hat from the opposite seat.

Sarah was exhausted and still had to face the wedding night which would set the pattern for their married life. Would he be conscious of the fact she had not much experience? Would he expect more than she understood about what happened between a man and woman? She pushed such thoughts from her mind. She could not worry about what might be when she needed to save her strength for the actual event when it arose.

Through the dusk of evening, a large home appeared. The man beside her sat straighter as he explained, "The staff shall come out to meet you. I have only been here once since returning to England so everything is new to me also. Griffin and Mrs. Griffin are the long-term, butler and housekeeper. Cook is new, but the stablemaster is the same one who taught me to ride."

"He must be ready to retire." Her words seemed to make him smile, and then she realized how she sounded. "Oh, not that you are very old, my lord, merely that you must have been very young when you first learned to ride."

"Quit while you are ahead and not make me feel like the ancient, I must appear to you."

Unsure what to say, she merely added, "Certainly, my lord, I look forward to meeting them all."

A footman stepped forward from the row of servants making a line from the drive to the front door. The viscount stepped down first then put out his hand to steady her as she made her way out and stood waiting to be introduced to the assembled group.

The older man, first in line, stepped forward and said, "My Lady, we welcome you to Wyngate and hope your time here shall be a happy one. We all are excited to have the family in residence again."

"I am excited to be here and look forward to learning about my new home. Thank you for the welcome, Griffin." Which earned her a slight smile as he turned toward his wife as she curtsied.

Sarah must have said the correct thing because the man began going down the line of servants calling them by name and telling her their positions in the household. She knew she would need to meet them a few more times before their names came readily to her. She found she was slightly distracted by the note she saw the butler palm to her husband and then the expression of concern which came across his face after reading it.

She was finally at the door, and the butler ushered her into a large foyer with black and white marble squares making a harlequin pattern across the floor. Turning, she realized there was something the viscount wished to say to her as they allowed the servants to return to their duties within the house.

"Something is the matter, my lord? You appear worried."

"Well, yes, I find I must return to London immediately. I am so sorry not to be here on your first night in your new home, but I feel this cannot wait…"

Placing her hand on his arm, she stated sincerely, "I understand the need for you to go. I shall find my way around, and the staff all seem eager to be of help to me. I shall go about learning my duties until you can return."

His gaze locked with hers, but then he lowered his head in a slight bow. "Thank you, my lady. I shall return as quickly as possible."

There was a knock on the door, and as the butler opened it, a smaller carriage with a two-man driving team stood waiting. Leaning toward her, he kissed her cheek and then turned to hurry toward the waiting conveyance.

*****

As Tony climbed into the carriage, he called out his order to go as quickly as possible. He wished he had not needed to take the enclosed carriage, but this time of year the weather was not to be trusted, and he hoped he could overcome the situation tonight and return tomorrow. These trips to London would become wearisome although he should have foreseen the problem arising.

"I shall push them as fast as I dare, my lord, but this lighter carriage will not hold to the roads like the larger traveling coach, and it shall be getting dark in less than an hour."

"Do the best you can, Cooper, but do not take chances. I am sure the emergency is an over-reach and not actually a life and death matter."

"Aye, my lord, I shall make good time."

Staring at the crumpled note in his hand, he went over the words again in his mind. *Please come. I need you immediately. M.*

Marguerite was always pleasantly supportive of this plan and had even encouraged his marriage to a woman unable to make her presence in society, especially London society. Although the older woman's attendance in the church this morning should have been a warning. When he glanced up at some sound which drew his attention to the pews and recognized her sitting there watching the ceremony, his first impulse was anger. After all they had agreed the two parts of his life were to remain separate. It was only fair—to both women.

Sarah should not need to face the woman who was his true partner while Marguerite did not need to see the young woman having his name and bearing his children. The woman everyone else would know as his chosen bride.

Worried something had befallen the woman he loved; he mentally urged the horses on and tried not to think of all the possibilities that would have made Marguerite call him to her side on the night of his wedding. A night he had hoped would set the pattern for many more to follow. At least until his wife became with child and he could return to his lover's side and resume enjoying the London season.

Pulling up outside the house he had rented for Marguerite, Tony sent the carriage on to his own stables down the block. The door was opened by the butler that came with the furnished house and then bowed him in.

"Where is she?"

"In her rooms, my lord." The man said without a blink or acknowledgement about the appropriateness of such a question.

Taking the steps two at a time, Tony rushed into the room they used to find Marguerite prostrate on the chaise lounge with a crumpled hankie in her fist. Red rimmed eyes turned to him accusingly. "You are finally here. I cannot believe you would leave me for so long."

After his break-neck trip back to London, he was not expecting to be called out on the time it took him to arrive. "I came as swiftly as I could, Marguerite. What is wrong? Are you ill? Did you fall?" His eyes skimmed appraisingly over her body clad in a translucent gown and robe and found nothing to alarm him. No signs any harm had befallen her.

"Only my heart. It is broken," she said theatrically before burying her head into her hands.

Expelling a long sigh, he realized she was physically unharmed and simply being dramatic over some slight she thought he had made. It was not the first time, and he felt these bouts of self-pity were coming more and more often. He tried to reassure her that he was not interested in the younger and many times, prettier ladies that threw themselves at him whenever they thought they could catch him in a compromising position. Again, he realized he had miscalculated the effect his marriage would have on his lover.

"Marguerite, come and talk to me. You knew I was to be married, and we agreed that you would not come or speak of it to anyone. Why did you change the plans?"

Sad, red-rimmed eyes peered up at him through tear spiked lashes. "I tried to find out more about the woman you decided to marry, and no one could remember what she looked like exactly. Oh, they remembered her as being pleasant and a good dancer, but nondescript. I hoped, I mean, I thought that meant she was not pretty or possibly even ugly." Then the tears flowed down the rouged cheeks. "But she is not, is she? She is lovely— and young—and perfectly acceptable."

"Come here, love." He pulled her into his arms as he sat next to her on the chaise. "I told you that you had nothing to fear from my marriage. Simply because she is not an ogre does not mean I shall fall in love with her. We have been together years, and I am as committed to you today as I was the first day I first saw you in St. Petersburg."

She patted his lapels and said quietly, "But she looked so young and fresh. I cannot believe she has given birth. Are you sure?"

"Yes, I am sure and I think she is too skinny. I do not believe she has had much money for food and that has affected her body."

Preening slightly, she straightened saying, "I found her shape a little too ingenue, but men…they sometimes have other tastes. You are not attracted to her? You are sure?"

"I find her attractive enough not to worry my children shall be anathema to society, but that is all. We discussed all of this already, my love. Now you have gotten yourself upset over nothing. I assure you."

Patting her eyes in a melodramatic fashion now that her tears had stopped, she said, "I was so upset and felt I had no one to talk to. How am I to live like this? Always waiting for you to return to me?" She tilted her head slightly. "Stay the night with me?"

"I may as well. It is too late or make that early to start back to Wyngate at this time, but Marguerite, you must let me do my duty, or this shall take much longer than we planned. It may take a few months and that puts off our plans that same amount of time."

"I know, but I felt so abandoned when I saw you at the altar. You both looked so, so in love."

Gently shaking her shoulder, he repeated, "You have nothing to worry about. I do not love her, nor does she love me. In fact, she thinks of me as being old."

"The woman is a fool then. You are the perfect age. The age I was when we met, and she has no idea how virile you are. A man who knows how to please a woman." She rubbed her hand across his arousal making itself known.

"And I intend to please my woman right now if you feel you can put up with making love with me."

"Of, course, *amore mio*," she whispered as she allowed the diaphanous negligée to fall to the floor.

CHAPTER FOUR

Sarah woke when the sun rose. The night before she had taken a meal in one of the several dining rooms not wishing to disappoint the staff by declaring herself too tired. Sitting in solitary grandeur, she was served a multi-course meal and the best wine she had ever drank. She met the cook again who came to make sure the food and presentation was acceptable to Sarah. Sarah had assured the robust woman she was more than pleased with all of it. She also complimented Griffin, Mrs. Griffin, and the footman who led her to her rooms.

Then finally alone, she sat limply into one of two chairs before the fireplace. All her strength had left her as she tried to remain the lady the staff was expecting their master to bring home. They had all been attentive to the point she was worried they would be disappointed once the shine wore off. Once they realized that such a house and lifestyle was completely alien to the way she had been living for the past two years. And even before that she had only seen such opulence when invited to the few private residences that did not vet their invitations too thoroughly.

The solitude gave her time to contemplate her room which was light and airy and newly decorated according to her husband. He had asked a professional to come to the estate and change everything. He jokingly said he did not wish any signs of his mother when he took his wife to bed. That it would result in a poor performance if not by embarrassing himself completely. Sarah was not sure what he was referring to, but could surmise. He wished his mind on his wife, and this room was surprisingly to Sarah's taste.

The cream white walls and yellow painted trim called out to her. The flowered coverlet and matching drapes made her think of early walks and the warmth of an English summer day. There were also fresh flowers making her realize there was some sort of indoor growing area. Perhaps she could have a small corner to grow her favorites. She would enjoy having a garden as she had at her little cottage. Growing things, both for their beauty and for the table, she found very rewarding.

The polished wood floor boasted a large patterned carpet which joined the areas together. That of the large dark wood bed to the sitting area where she found herself now. Two interior doors were on one wall. She guessed the one closest to the corner was the dressing room while the other she assumed led to her husband's sleeping quarters. The room now empty due to the secretive note he received upon their arrival.

Was there really some emergency? Other than his paramour, he had no business she knew. He had told her he left the estate in the hands of a long-standing steward, Fellner, who she was yet to meet. The viscount was not interested in commerce of any sort, but she had honestly not cared that he seemingly abandoned her on her wedding night.

Her husband's immediate departure meant a quiet, worry-free evening for her. Putting off the inevitable gave her more time to get used to the place. She could look at that large bed and not find it any more intimidating than any of the other furniture. She found herself calmed and free of the nerves she felt she would have faced otherwise.

Today she was free to investigate the rooms, at least the immediate ones in use, and perhaps a short walk in the gardens she could see from her window. A side garden probably reached by way of a parlor on the east side. Possibly a parlor she could adopt as her own where she could spend most of her time when not in the nursery.

Having turned down the help of a personal maid, explaining she had one arriving any day, Sarah dressed quickly. Pushing in the ends of her *fichu,* she studied herself in the full- length mirror. Satisfied, although knowing she did not appear as a viscountess should, she opened the door between hers and her husband's room.

If she thought her room light and gay, the master's sleeping chamber was just the opposite. Dark paneling encircled the room higher than her shoulders topped with a dark leather pasted as high as the dark wood cove molding. A gold painted ceiling held a large plaster medallion from which hung a many candled chandelier. The tiled fireplace was cold and dark also, but she knew it was not from a faulty flue. This room with its brooding bed hangings and dark plaid covered chairs was a man's domain. It shouted masculinity and stay-out to any female who unknowingly may have wandered into it.

Was this how her husband wished things? Was this room to his taste or that of other Viscounts Wyndom? She would accept the 'keep-out sign' and remain on her side of the door. It was not as if they had the kind of relationship where she would be expected to seek him out in the night. She returned to her own room and felt a heaviness lift from her.

Already in better spirits, though still curious, Sarah went out to the hallway peeking into every room with an open door which seemed to be most of them on this floor. She found mostly sleeping chambers, a couple of smallish parlors with sleeping chambers off of them, and a nursery including rooms for a nursemaid and nanny. It was located farthest from the master's suite, but she felt it would work. She could always move to a closer room after the babies were born. After all, the viscount could not possibly wish to stay once there was a young child in residence. Surely the lures of London and his paramour would be more than enough cause for the man to leave.

Leave and allow her to live the life she planned. Taking care of her children and puttering in the garden, bringing the children with her to enjoy the weather and fresh country air.

Once downstairs, she startled a dozing footman sitting on a chair in the foyer.

He brushed the hair out of his eyes while stumbling over his words. "Oh, my lady, I did not expect to see you so early. I am to call Griffin immediately."

"No, wait on that if you will. I am merely getting my bearings and shall go down to the kitchens and have a word with Cook. No need to disturb the Griffins or their routine."

She could tell he was unsure of whose directions to follow.

"If that is how you wish it, my lady." He bowed and returned to the chair slowly.

"Do not worry, Tom, I shall let Griffin know this was my wish."

She did not know if it was her words or the fact she knew his name, but the young man's face cleared of worry, and he gave a small smile in return as she turned to find the closest set of stairs leading downward.

Not wishing to surprise the staff and possibly cause an accident with spilled hot water or some other disaster, she found the tweeny getting the coal shuttles ready to be taken upstairs.

"Meg, is it not?" The young girl of about ten years gaped from where she kneeled and nodded, her mouth open in shock at seeing Sarah below stairs.

Jumping up, the young girl gave a wobbly curtsy saying, "Yes'm. Can I help you find somethin'?"

"I was going to talk to Cook, is all. Go on with your duties. I did not mean to interrupt."

"No, my lady, you can go wherever you wish."

"Then I think I shall just go along this way. My nose shall lead me to the kitchen, I think." Sarah gave the girl a conspiratorial wink and continued toward the warmth and sounds of pans clanging together.

Mrs. Springstead, the cook, had heard her as Sarah thought she would and was prepared when Sarah entered the kitchen.

"My lady, did you wish breakfast? There is a bell-pull that…"

"I know about the bell-pulls, but I wished to come down and speak with you directly."

"Yes, my lady, anything you wish, my lady."

Sarah knew this was probably unusual and that this staff had been left alone for quite a long time so they did things the way they liked. She was not going to change that. The kitchen, from what she could see, was pristine. No mice droppings or signs of infestation. She noticed an indent on a pillow near the hearth indicating a cat's presence which usually insured no rodents.

"I would like to see how you make a meal, if you do not mind. I have always been fascinated by what goes into making as nice a meal as I was served last evening."

An expression of doubt crossed the woman's face. "Are you sure, my lady? I don't think…"

"I have some experience of cooking over an open hearth, but nothing as lavish as what you provided. I would like to make soup and take it to those on the estate who are unable to get out. Possibly bring them blankets or items they need but cannot afford at this time. If there are any new babies," her voice softened automatically, "I am quite partial to little ones and the mothers are always in need of clothing and such."

They must have been the correct words because the stout woman uncrossed her arms from over her ample stomach and nodded. "The master married a right one then, after all. We had heard things about…well, you never mind. I shall show you what I've got going right now. A porridge for the staff, who shall gather for each meal, but always leavin' someone on duty at all times. The valet and your lady's maid shall be fed down here at the same time you and the master take your meals since they are often busy above stairs when the rest of us eat."

"I passed a room with a long table. Is that the room the staff uses?"

"Aye, and when we have a full staff then we eat in turns. The butler and housekeeper have a room offin' that hall, and I have one behind the chimney. Most of the others are housed on the top floor. Mrs. Griffin can tell you more about them although the kitchen seems to be a gathering place most times."

Glancing around, Sarah said, "I can understand why. Is that the porridge, I smell?"

"Oh, yes, my lady. I best see to it before it scalds down." The mature woman stepped to the large pot hanging over the red coals and stirred vigorously. "Now I started with a good pitcher full of water…"

****

Sarah was glad she had invaded the kitchen. After a short time, Cook had forgotten who she was speaking to and told Sarah all sorts of interesting things about the staff. It was not surprising that most of them had ties to the people living on the estate, in the village, or in service to the Wyndom family.

She took note whenever an older person was spoken of and particularly about any woman who had recently given birth. After going through the process herself, she knew a new mother needed all the rest she could get. Keeping a baby fed was not easy, and if there were other little ones needing food and care, Sarah wished to help. Dropping off a meal for a few days and making sure there was food available for the rest of the time did not seem to be a hardship. She knew Lucy would help the same as she had when Sarah was in confinement.

Cook began a soup that would be served at luncheon while Sarah ate a poached egg on bread she had toasted over the embers. "This is all I need in the morning along with a pot of tea. I am not sure about the days my husband is here."

"The young master always ate large meals, I was told, but his valet said now he only wishes scrambled eggs, a piece of meat, and bread. Said he was not used to big English breakfasts any more since living on the continent. I don't expect to get too much to do in the mornings." It sounded as if the woman was taking their not eating breakfast as a personal affront.

"Well, that gives us time to put together the baskets I shall be delivering once I get the lay of the land. The woman you said used to be a nursemaid here shall be the first followed by the family where the new birth just occurred."

"That be over a week ago, my lady."

"And I hope she hasn't been overwhelmed caring for the wee one as well as the two others. It sounds like I arrived right in time."

"Aye, mayhaps you have, my lady. I shall get them two baskets down from the shelf, and then we'll see what we can glean from the pie-safe to send with you."

Smiling that things were going so well Sarah followed the woman down to the cooler basement and helped select items to fill the baskets.

Striding into the interior of the house with a basket in each hand Sarah almost ran into a man coming down the hall. His face was practically buried in a small ledger book.

"Oh, I am sorry," she said automatically as the baskets preceded her into the hall.

The man stopped and looked her up and down then said, "Who are you? I don't remember authorizing any new hires. Did Mrs. Griffin hire you?"

He seemed put out that Sarah was there and that he had not been conferred with first although even his firmed lips did not hide the fact, he was extremely attractive. Dark blond hair was swept back from his face and worn a little long, but not long enough for a que. Silver blue eyes took in her appearance, and she thought his eyes dilated just a fraction when his gaze reached her face.

"Um, no, I arrived, um, with Viscount Wyndom."

He scoffed. "Well, you had better get into proper livery and make sure you keep out of the family living quarters. I do not think the new viscount would appreciate getting nearly run down by one of his servants."

"He is not here right now. Was called back to London as soon as he arrived."

He raised to his full height which appeared to be over six feet and peering down his straight nose at her said, "The help never speak about the family's business nor comment upon their whereabouts and goings on. Do I make myself clear?"

He was so full of himself she could not help pulling his other leg. Curtsying, she nodded, "Yes, my lord. I understand, my lord."

Rolling his eyes, he said very slowly as if speaking to someone of very little intellect, "I am not a lord. I am the steward who runs the household and lands of the estate. You may call me Mister Fellner. And I should know you as...?"

Waiting a moment trying to see if she could extricate herself before he realized just who he was conversing with she said meekly, "Sarah?"

"Well, Sarah, as I said previously, please see Mrs. Griffin for a maid's livery and remain in the servant's quarters unless doing a job that requires you to come into the family's area."

She thought another curtsy was called for as he continued on his way to the room, she thought to be the steward's office since it opened onto the side garden. The same one she wished to cultivate if given the chance.

Hurrying upstairs, she found her cape and hat and descended hoping not to run into the steward. She was not sure if the man had a sense of humor although it seemed he took his position there and the family's privacy very much to heart. She did not wish him to think she had been mocking him,\ but now was unsure how to announce her position without embarrassing him. She felt it was partly her own fault for not dressing like a viscountess. As soon as Lucy arrived, they would be able to sort through the dresses she had stored. After altering any as needed, Sarah would be a much more presentable lady.

Following the path the cook told her to take, Sarah would come to the cottage covered with rose vines where the elderly woman, Nanny Wright, resided. Sarah walked through the archway with a few die-hard pink roses still clinging to the dead looking briar covered vines. Sarah wondered if the old woman was even home. There were leaves blown up against the door proving it had not been used in a while, but she knocked anyway.

"Mrs. Wright? I am here to bring you some soup and ask if you need anything."

No answer, but Sarah thought there was the sound of a chair hitting the floor. Could the old woman have fallen trying to answer the door? Should she enter and call out again so she did not frighten the woman if she were inside?

The door was unlocked. Sarah pushed it wide so as to show anyone inside she was alone and had only baskets for weapons. A movement across the room indicated the body of a woman lying on the clean floorboards and a hand waving her to enter.

Running over and kneeling, Sarah said, "Oh, my dear, are you hurt? How can I help?"

"I am a foolish old woman and thought I could walk

without my cane. I was shown up for my hubris," the old woman said with more vigor than Sarah thought possible from the diminutive woman lying in front of her. The woman was already trying to stand, and Sarah realized which leg must be her weakest and moved to that side to help raise her. Bending, Sarah picked up the chair which had fallen making the noise she heard from outside.

"I would like to make it to the chair by the fire. It is very comfortable, and the viscountess gave it to me when I retired or rather when she retired me. I always felt I had more to give if there had been more children."

Sarah made sure the older woman was sitting securely and her ankle, now appearing bruised, was resting on a low footstool.

"Do you wish your shawl? I see the fire has gone out, and it shall take a while to build it back up."

"There's wood outside leaning against the cottage if you will bring some in. And possibly some pine cones as starters."

Finding the wood pile easily, Sarah filled her arms with split logs and her hands with pine cones. Enough to leave the extras by the side of the hearth for another time. Returning inside, she laid the wood down and began stacking them using the pinecones and dried needles as tinder. This took Sarah very little time as she was well versed in starting fires. She never had enough fuel to allow a fire to burn all night in the cottage. She had slept with Topher in her bed to assure he stayed warm.

The kindling caught, and she leaned back on her heels. "There, that should warm you quickly. Once the sun goes down it could turn into a chilly night."

Kind, pale blue eyes stared at Sarah. "Now that we have the necessities covered, who may I thank for this serendipitous arrival and rescue?"

"Um, I have come from the manor with soup and bread, honey and tea leaves. I was not sure what else you needed, but I thought this was a beginning."

"A beginning, my lady? What have I done to earn such bounty?"

"Oh, you know who I am?"

"Not until you began speaking. I know a London accent when I hear it, plus after all these years, who else would come worrying about me?"

"Well, Cook mentioned you living here alone and thought you would appreciate the effort. She packed up the baskets for the most part."

"And here you are giving her the credit that should belong to you. I see my boy kept some of the sense he showed years ago. How is the lad?"

Realizing the woman in front of her was speaking about the six foot plus man Sarah was married to, she had to think about her answer. How was her husband? She did not rightly know. He was well dressed, well educated, handsome, and had a sense of power about him, but was that something she could tell an old retainer even if the woman had changed the man's diapers?

"He is well. We married recently, and I am still getting to know him. He seems nice enough."

"Hmm, nice enough, is he? A damning recommendation from a wife, I can tell you. Where is he and why did he allow you out here on your first visit to Wyngate alone?" Her pale eyes seemed to see to the bottom of Sarah's soul.

"The viscount was called back to London, and I felt in need of doing something besides learning which room we hold formal dinners in."

"Feisty, are you? Not sure how well Anthony shall take to that, but, of course, I don't know him any longer. He was still a child when he was sent off to school. Not so young that he still wet the bed, but not old enough to need a straight blade, either."

"I do not think of myself as feisty. I do not bulk at rules or what is expected of me, but I have found myself on a path I did not plan and making the best of it."

"Now that is an intriguing statement, my lady."

"I did not intend it to be. Let us get this soup warmed and perhaps a pot of tea? I will not leave until you are fed and cared for. At least enough that you can stand on that ankle."

"Oh, this thing has been a thorn in my side for years. I first thought it was gout, but the doctor tells me otherwise. I am to use the cane in case it gives out on me, but I fail to see the sense of needing it to cross my own home." The woman looked at Sarah trying not to laugh since that is exactly what happened. "All right. That old coot of a doctor may be right."

Sarah turned to a sideboard to find a small pot in which to heat the soup.

"You're going to have to tell me at some point how a viscountess can start a fire from needles and twigs and knows her way around a cottage kitchen. This is not something you just learned."

"No, I have talents now that I did not have as a debutant, but we do not have time today to learn about one another. I would like to know more about my husband as a boy, even as an infant."

"I think that is possible. Perhaps you shall return for tea when I can serve you proper like. I feel badly that you found me in such straits." The old woman peered around the cottage as if viewing it from Sarah's eyes.

"I am glad I arrived when I did, or you may still be lying on the floor with the dark and cold setting in. I have items for the Donner family, or I would stay longer."

"Oh, yes, that poor girl. Her husband seems to not miss a chance to prove his manhood. This is her third child in as many years. She doesn't even get a chance to wean one before she is caught by another." The harrumph that followed told Sarah all she needed to know about what the old nanny thought about such goings on. Sarah wondered what the older woman would think if that was Sarah's future as well. It had not been spoken of nor addressed in the contract as to how many and how often she would be expected to bear a child. Her first had taken only the one time so how quickly could she plan on another if they lived together for weeks at a time as planned?

"I think that is why I was given food in her basket. I shall make sure there is enough in her cupboards daily. The young are the heart's blood of any estate. The people living here must make enough to feed their family, or they shall leave to work in the manufactories sprouting up like hogweed in the north."

"Now you're sounding more like a viscount's wife. A woman worried about her husband's estate and the people who live on it." The woman nodded in approval and sniffed appreciatively at the warming soup.

"I am a viscount's wife and am trying to find my way."

"You already have, my lady. You know exactly how to be a viscountess, and I am so glad my boy knew to marry you."

Smiling, Sarah poured the water on the tea leaving

it to steep while she dipped a bowl of soup for her hostess.

****

"Oh, Lucy, I am so glad you have come. I saw the loneliest woman I have ever seen in my life."

"Who are you speaking of?" Her friend stared at her aghast. "Someone working here in the house?"

"No, one of the tenant farmer's wives. She is barely twenty and has three young children. One of them less than two weeks old." Sarah sat on one of the chairs pointing to the other.

Lucy took the chair offered. "What do you think we should do? I mean, it is not as if he is beating her. You cannot expect to step between a man and his wife and their marriage bed. Not out here in the countryside. A woman has even fewer choices here."

Feeling helpless, Sarah nodded. "I know and she seems tended to, but the weight of taking care of all those children as well as the household duties…"

"I know. We had Mum to help and discuss things with. We were never all alone with Topher on our own."

Sarah knew her friend was right and knew she owed both of the Coop women more than she could ever repay. "We had your mother, and I had you. I was never alone unless I wished to be, and this poor woman has no one to ask for help. She is not from around here, and her husband is in the fields all day."

"I can take some time and make friends with her. You can send extra food and possibly some baby clothes. She probably does not have any extras since she already has two in dresses."

"No, I did not see much besides what the children were wearing. A few swaddling cloths hanging out to dry. The children were barefoot and in this cold. I did not like to leave her like that, but she seemed happier after we spoke for a while, and she became used to me being in her home. There was a large pile of wood, so it is not as if the husband is not minding his family, but I think food is scarce. She felt embarrassed at not having anything to offer me for refreshment."

Lucy took Sarah's hand. "That must have been difficult for you. I know how soft your heart is and how you hate to see anyone in distress."

Sarah patted Lucy's hand with her free one. "You are a dear, dear friend and you know me so well, but now that we are aware of their plight, we can rectify it. I think we must be careful not to step on her husband's pride. He seems a hard worker, but this last year, from what I understand, was not very good here. First spring rains flooded the fields and floated the seed away leaving some to mold in the ground and then months of drought. All the people here may have a hard winter. We may need to appeal to the viscount and see if he could lessen the amount of crops he takes as rent."

Lucy's eyes widened. "Do you think he shall? I mean it must be a lot of money I am not sure…"

"Neither am I. I suppose I should talk to the steward and see if such a thing is even possible before I ask the viscount. I have met Fellner, and he seems capable."

"He's so handsome. I heard about him as soon as I arrived today. I think I was being warned off. Once I explained I was married, then all the maids were telling me how wonderful he was and how kind his eyes were."

"Hmm, I am not sure he shall look upon me with 'kind eyes', but since we live in the same house, he cannot ignore me. This time I shall meet him as the viscountess." Sarah stood to search her wardrobe. "Where is that peach colored day dress with the lace neckline?"

****

Sarah really should have explained who she was as soon as she had run into Fellner in the hallway. He may not wish to spend any time with her let alone hear her out about the tenants' needs and how they can be met. Tapping on the door, she waited while holding her breath. How could she tell him who she was without making him feel the fool?

The door opened, and the steward stepped back bowing politely. "My lady, how may I be of service to you?"

Swallowing the explanations and apologies, she entered and peered around a very neat office with shelves of ledgers and others of brochures and pamphlets all dealing with sheep and cattle it seemed. "I see you discovered my identity."

"I had not realized it was a game, or I would have thought more deeply. Finding a young woman coming from the kitchen carrying baskets led me to believe my eyes and not see further. I do apologize."

"No, it is I who should be apologizing. You asked me who I was, and I should have said the truth right then. The fact that you assumed me to be a servant brought home my poor dress choice and the fact I had not waited for my lady's maid to dress my hair or make me presentable. I am very used to my own company and have forgotten a lady never leaves her chambers in less than perfect toilet."

"It would be ungentlemanly of me to speak upon how my lady was dressed, but I did jump to a conclusion where I could see it difficult to escape from. Either way, I was going to feel and appear less than sterling."

"Can we forget that brief moment in time and begin again?" Putting out her hand to shake his, she said, "Good morning. I am Lady Wyndom, but you may call me, Sarah, since we may run into one another many times throughout my time here."

"You may call me anything you wish, but I hardly think the viscount shall wish me to address you as anything besides 'my lady'."

"If today is anything to go by, I do not think the viscount shall be here long enough to know. I believe he plans on living most of the time in London while I enjoy the country and fresh air."

"Well, then London's loss is Wyngate's gain."

"Well put. Now, if I may, I have a request to see the books regarding the harvest this year and possibly compare it to past harvests. I have heard there were problems with the rain this summer?"

If the man was surprised by her inquisitiveness, he did not show it. He pulled down several ledgers neatly marked as to the year covered and flipped through the pages reaching about the same place in each book.

"There are records for everything harvested, how much went into the communal barns and lofts and how much went to the estate as rent. We work on a percentage rather than a set amount. It is only fair, my lady."

"I agree that is the fairest way, but is it possible to alter that amount?"

"You wish to charge the tenant's more, my lady?" She could tell without words he thought her greedy in the highest degree.

"No, I wish to see if there was a way to charge less.

Allow the farmers to keep more of their harvest since it was such a poor year. There is no way I could enjoy any food on my table knowing it meant the farmers' families were going without."

She raised her eyes from the lists she had been reading to make her point to the man who probably was paid by the amount of harvest he collected. "Do you understand?"

"I do, my lady. I shall look at the amounts of each item and see if there are places, we can alter our share. Of course, the viscount would need to approve any changes."

"Um, I have a household account. My husband said I am in control of everything if I so desire. Do you think there is anything there which we can lessen or cut out completely?"

"Not of past years since the budget was set to cover the minimum number of servants and a closed house. This new budget was an estimation of your needs. I can show you that ledger if you wish, and you may take it to study. It is all very straightforward and you may have more of an idea about the costs for entertaining and such."

Since she knew there would be no entertaining and that the viscount would be gone as soon as she knew she was with child, perhaps there was money not needed for the household without letting anyone go.

"I do and I shall accept the ledger to work on tonight. I do not think the viscount shall be home yet since he would not have reached London much before daybreak."

She accepted the smaller book he handed her and turned away as he bowed. He had remained standing the entire time they spoke.

Of course, he would have. As a gentleman, he could not sit down until she did so and approved his sitting as well. There were many things she had forgotten in the past two years. All the little things that seemed so important her first season were lessened. Her priorities and her desires were much more mundane than when she was a child. And nineteen seemed like a child no matter how fast one had to grow up.

CHAPTER FIVE

The following morning after having stayed up late studying and making notes where Sarah thought the budget could be trimmed, an idea came to her as to how to bond the tenants and those living nearby to the estate again. A man will not move his family away from everything they have ever known. Not unless it was the only way to keep the family from starving.

It had been the note about the holiday entertainments and their tentative costs. It seemed like an extravagant amount for only her. She was sure the viscount would spend the time in London with his lady friend where there would be parties and special entertainments as well as balls. Sarah was sure he would leave her for several weeks which would cover the new year, as well.

It was a mere two months away, and Sarah thought about how to get the tenants and villagers to celebrate the holidays together. Boxing day would be a good time to reward the tenants and household staff at the same time since so many were related anyway. Perhaps a Hogmanay ritual for the new year could be held. The vicar should be consulted, also. Encouraged to add his blessing to the meals and gatherings.

It all boiled down to costs and how much she could eke from the household budget. There were so many things she wished to do and all before the end of the year.

Excitement rushed through her body just as she heard the front door open.

Griffin's voice called out politely, "My lord, it is good to see you again. I hope your trip was not too strenuous."

"No, Griffin, merely things needing to be put in place. I shall be home for the next few weeks."

"Good to hear it, my lord."

"Is my wife awake, yet?"

"Oh, yes, sir. She is in the back parlor which she has made her own."

"Thank you, I shall take myself to her then."

It was barely a minute before she saw her door open further. She had not stirred from her seat as she moved pins on the pillow in front of her as the bobbins clattered near her feet.

"I see you have found a room that suits you very well." He looked about the brightly sunlit room nodding at the fresh flowers and polished surfaces. "I do not recall this room, at all."

"I do not think it was used much, my lord. I took the initiative of moving some French furniture from other rooms and the attic to furnish it. The draperies and paint were already the cream, and I added the gold and white and light gray that was in the Aubusson carpet."

"It is charming, and I can see where it shall become a favorite."

"Yes, the morning light is good even this time of year, and the garden is right outside. I plan on using that as my personal garden if that is agreeable."

"Certainly, you shall be spending your time here, so do as you wish. I am sure the staff and Fellner shall help with any needs."

"They have been very helpful, I assure you. I am feeling quite comfortable here already."

Her words seemed to have pleased him as he smiled and sat in one of several gold painted chairs trusting it to take his weight.

"I was unsure what I would find upon my return here. You have every right to be less than pleased with my rapid trip back to London on our wedding night."

"I assume you needed to leave, and I am not in a position to feel one way or another about it. I secured a good night's sleep, investigated the house, visited with a couple of the cottagers, and set up this room. As you can see, I have been keeping busy learning what my position shall require of me…besides furnishing you with your heir, I mean." She smiled showing him she did not find anything out of order with her life so far.

"I appreciate your sufferance, but from now on I plan on being a husband. I have made arrangements to continue on here for an indefinite period."

She knew he meant until she was with child, and she nodded in agreement. After all, that was what she planned on and as soon as she was with child, the viscount would return to London and his life there. Then she could spend more time with Topher and Mrs. Coop and possibly even move Topher into the house.

"I should let you get on with your, um, is that lace making?"

"Yes, my lord. I am quite good at it and am making collars to give as gifts at Christmas."

"My, I have not even thought of Christmas yet. You are very organized."

"I know how quickly time passes, so I hate to waste any. I thought we would keep to country hours for meals and not dress formally for dinner unless you wish it otherwise."

"No, I find changing clothes so many times a day, unless one has been out riding, a nuisance. I brought Harvey back with me, though, so I shall need to find something else to keep him occupied."

"Hmm, does he sew?"

He seemed surprised by the question. "I assume so since I know he has mended several shirts and such. Does a marvelous job with my boots... Why do you ask?"

"Oh, I was simply wondering, my lord. If he is at loose ends, I may have a few jobs he can do."

"I shall inform him of such this evening." Standing, he looked at her with an expression she was unable to read. "We shall begin our lives as man and wife tonight, if that is agreeable to you."

She glanced away, unable to hold his gaze in her shyness. "Certainly, my lord. I shall await you in my chamber."

As he left, her gaze followed his back.

****

Carrying the decanter and two empty sherry glasses, Tony knocked lightly before turning the doorknob to enter his wife's room. The fire light played upon Sarah's face as she turned toward him expectantly.

"I thought you would enjoy a glass of sherry." He set the glasses on the small table between the chairs and filled them a little more than half full. Handing her one, he took the other, both drinking at the same time.

"Hmm, this is the first time I have had sherry, my lord." Her tongue came out to lick the sweet liquor remaining on her top lip. He found his gaze remained there even as her mouth turned into a smile. She seemed to be waiting for him to say something.

She wore a voluminous long-sleeved nightgown which was tied with a ribbon secured around her neck. Bare toes peeked from the hemline, and she reminded him of a young girl rather than a married woman who had given birth already in her life.

"I find this one very much to my taste. I was lucky enough to find it hidden away in the wine cellar when I last visited. It was brought in by my father."

"Well, I cannot say as to its quality, but I find it pleasant, as well."

"I thought we should talk first. Before we continue tonight."

She nodded, but her gaze studied the flames as if she were shy of him and what they were about to do—consummate their marriage. He understood there would be some hesitancy since they were basically strangers. He had hoped their trip to Wyngate had formed a bond, but then his unexplained rapid escape to London ended that closeness. He could tell this afternoon when he first arrived and then the monosyllabic answers during their dinner sustained his unease. If this persisted, he did not know if he could continue. Not tonight at least. He needed her to meet him on some level, or he would feel as if he were taking advantage of the woman in the basest of ways.

"Sarah, I must apologize again about disappearing on our wedding night. I think our consummating our marriage would have been easier on both of us if I had simply remained."

Her head swiveled toward him. "I am not in a displeasure at your actions. We are here together now, and I am aware of what must be done even if I do not have the experience, you may think I have."

He refilled her glass and then his own as he asked, "What do you mean by that?

Her gaze returned to staring into the flames. "It was the last night Lieutenant Geoffrey was in London. He had received his orders to go to one of the seaports to be deployed. We had only known each other a few weeks, but both of us knew it was love. He gave me his ring as a promise to return and marry me. We took a few minutes to sneak into the garden, and he kissed me."

Tony allowed her to get her words thought out as he waited patiently.

"He was so distraught at the thought of leaving me, saying he feared that as soon as he was gone, I would forget him. I promised him that I would not do that. That I had accepted his ring as his troth, and he should take that acceptance as mine."

Again, her words stopped, but she remained staring into the flames as if remembering that evening all over again. Possibly the cool air on her skin and the scent of the summer roses...

"He, he wished more from me and I was so in love, so worried for his safety I allowed him to take liberties—and it seemed right. I was going to marry him, so what was the harm?"

He poured over the words. "And that was the extent of your, um, knowledge? A hasty mating in the back garden?" He wondered if his crass words would get a harsh reply, but she seemed lost in memories.

"Yes, it was hasty, and we returned to the family parlor as if nothing momentous had occurred between us." She turned to face him and seemed back in the room with him both in mind and body. "So, as I said, I am not exactly experienced with being with a man, but I cannot see that it shall be a problem for getting with child."

"No, your lack of experience is not what worries me at this moment. It is the fact you have only had one involvement with a man and that time you got with child. Losing both the child and its father must be on your mind at this moment and possibly when I take you to wife. I only wish two of us in that bed."

She nodded as if she understood and turned back to watching the flames with a far-off expression on her face.

He spoke decisively. "We shall try again tomorrow. I mean to continue as I begin so I wish it to be right. I am your husband, and I wish a wife who shall welcome me not merely put up with me. We shall dine together tomorrow evening."

He left her sitting without another comment and found himself in his empty room which felt cool after his wife's cozily warm one. Now how was he to put himself to sleep? He had left his sherry in the other bed chamber and would die before retrieving it with an excuse and apology for bothering her again.

****

Dinner had been strained. The longer this consummation was postponed, the longer and wider the gap between his wife and him seemed to become. He should have stayed last night and proceeded as he had planned. Now the specter of her lieutenant would be there again tonight as a reminder of why nothing occurred between them last night. It was like a never-ending cause and effect.

As they ended dinner, he walked with her toward the

parlor but stopped her before entering. "I certainly do not wish to prolong this with taking tea. Shall you agree to retire for the night so we may have some privacy to discuss the apparition hanging between us?"

"Certainly, my lord, whatever is your preference."

"Tonight, I shall pull rank and ask that it be so. The rest of our marriage rests on our being able to come to some agreement over this…"

"I am agreeable, my lord. You have, but to inform me of your intentions so I am prepared. I shall attend to things and send Lucy home."

"Then I shall be with you shortly." He bowed and hoped none of the servants noticed the hushed words which sounded anything besides lover-like to his own ears.

He found her sitting in the chair in front of the fire and her eyes, a dark shade of green tonight, met his gaze as soon as he entered.

"Sarah, what has been bothering you all day? Can we be honest with one another as we were on the trip here? Is it your lieutenant? Do you think of him?"

"No, I mean, I do, but not in conjunction with this. Christopher is dead, and that shall not change. I came to grips with that fact years ago."

He thought she would not answer and then inhaling deeply she began again, "How can we do this without more between us?" Shaking her head, she seemed to be trying to remember anything she could about such things. As an unmarried girl, there probably had not been much. "How do I lay with you knowing your thoughts shall be of another just as you accuse me of doing with Christopher?"

How to explain his placing himself in two lives?

Two separate worlds so to speak. "I made this decision to wed with the sole thought of having a wife who would love my children and take care of them as I would expect. It was not meant to demean or hurt you in any manner— including making you feel less than my wife."

She nodded as if listening and understanding. "I shall not imagine I am with Christopher, either. It would lessen what the two of us had together even if you and I are now husband and wife. I see we need to keep the present separate from the past. In your case, the Wyngate separate from the London."

Nodding, he wished to make sure she understood his thinking. Needed her not to feel diminished in their marriage by not being in love with one another.

"I did not marry you to cause you some sort of penance. I wish us to enjoy our time together. I wish you to feel what every woman should feel in her marriage bed with her husband, but it is between you and I. I need to keep the two separate, just as you surmised."

"But what shall you tell her? How shall you explain?" Those moss-colored eyes sought his for some elusive answer.

"She will not ask, and I will not say."

"Then I think we should get on with things." Standing, she asked, "Do you wish me to be in bed?"

He searched her face and found no anger or resentment, no hurt or despair. She was accepting this as his wife, and they would go on from there. From tonight she would be his wife in all the ways, but one. He would not love this woman in a way a husband would—and she would not love him as a wife does. It was as he thought it would be and felt satisfied; they both understood the rules.

Watching as she climbed into bed still wearing that voluminous gown, he blew out all the candles, but the one next to the bed. Removing his robe leaving him naked, he slid in the side opposite the one his wife entered. How strange it felt to be next to a woman who was not Marguerite. How strange to respond to that same woman without the need of a severe talk to himself about duty and need of an heir. Perhaps the male body was more adaptable than one would like. Perhaps more than he thought his would be, at least.

He felt at odds as he could feel her waiting, lying rigid and tempering her breaths so as to not make a sound. What was she waiting for? Did she still fear him or the act? Was she in fact thinking of her lieutenant?

Finding the edge of the gown, he rucked it up to her waist without touching her in any way. His manhood appreciated the fact that she was bare and open to him, but something felt off. Something was not as Tony had planned it to be. Touching the soft curls between her legs, he felt her tense and stiffen even more. Entering her intimately with one finger told him she was warm, but not ready for his taking.

"I am not doing this right."

"It felt like it was right to me." Her first words to him since moving to the bed, and he felt there may yet be hope for them.

"Well, I assure you that is not the case. I could make our time together much better, and I intend to do so from now on."

"That sounds rather apprehensive."

"No, it will not be. It should have been something I thought about before now. To be honest, I had, but thought you would feel more comfortable if I visited your bed and then left without any other conversation between us. I feel that was a mistake which I shall rectify."

"I do not understand. Did I do something wrong? Please tell me…"

"No, as I said, I did something wrong. I am your husband and expect this to be a welcome time between us. To be pleasant and shared and a consummation of our marriage. A promise to one another."

"I, I would like that, I think. I wish our children to be conceived without rancor or hostility. Without regret."

"Exactly. May I remove this thing?"

"Yes, it is the only one I had, and it is left over from my pre-adolescent days at a finishing school." Hearing the humor in her voice, he relaxed as he pulled the offending garment over her head and let it fall to the floor.

"There." Leaning over he kissed her tentatively finding her less than timid in answer to his unasked question. His tongue followed the seam of her lips, and she opened her mouth to his, accepting his thorough search before responding in the same manner.

His hands stroked from her shoulder to her hip and back again before focusing on one breast as it peaked beneath his palm. There were no words spoken between them, but he read her assent by the little wiggles and the way her body pressed up into his hand. As his mouth covered one nipple, he heard the first of several whimpers which made his erection ache to fill her.

This time when his finger entered her, she was not only warm she was wet with her need, her wish. His body's reaction was a strong urge to press into her to prove he was virile and she was ready. He positioned himself over her as she spread her legs to give him room to nest there, but he could not hold back. Penetrating her for the first time he gazed into her eyes as they stared at one another.

"I don't know what to do," she confessed as if in apology.

"That is all right. I do." He placed a splayed hand beneath her fanny and as he penetrated, she lifted her hips to his. Her eyes closed. Another whimper and she met his next plunge without hesitation.

He was inflamed and pursued his own movements accepting hers as she gave them always accompanied by those little whimpers, silent pleas for more.

Her legs wrapped around his hips, and he held onto her buttocks as her hands held his head to hers, their lips in constant contact as he felt her muscles tighten around him. He felt her throb with her final orgasm.

When their breathing quieted, he waited to break the spell that still held them in its thrall.

"Shall you tell her?"

He did not have to ask whom she was speaking of. He knew she was thinking of Marguerite.

"What happens between us as a married couple is no one's business, but ours. She knew that going into this and will not question my actions."

"But that was so much more than merely joining to beget an heir. That was…some sort of mystical mating. Something I never conjured in my wildest imaginings."

"Nature has her own way of making sure there is a future generation. Making our coupling enjoyable is merely one of them. I am glad to find we are so compatible." He did not wish to think too deeply, too much about their coming together and his ultimate orgasm. Possibly impregnating his wife and making any further coupling unnecessary. He did not wish to think about that. Not right now when his body still hummed from his time with her.

Finally, exiting from the warm covers, he slid the chilly silken robe back on. He needed to find some semblance of normalcy. Find a path to their original plan.

"I prefer to find you in bed naked with your hair untied and waiting for me the evenings I am at home." Then tying the belt in place, he left through the adjoining bedroom door.

****

In the morning, her husband knocked on the still open door adjoining their rooms. He poked his head in with a welcoming smile.

"I shall be spending the day with my steward. If I had thought about it sooner, I would have canceled. I still could."

Sarah met him with the same neutral spirit she meant to continue giving nothing away about how she felt after last night.

"No, my lord, please do not do so on my account. I, too, have duties that shall take up most of my day." She hoped he would not ask what those duties were since she was not a very good liar. Not telling someone something was not the same as telling a lie so she could fabricate and still look herself in the eyes in a mirror. Something she had been asserting if only to herself every day since her wedding.

He lowered his gaze so she could not read his thoughts. "I shall see you at dinner then. Country hours then?"

"Yes, unless you wish it otherwise."

Smiling, he gave her a wicked grin, "No, the earlier we dine the earlier we can retire…"

She covered her head with the sheet unable to meet his gaze. When she allowed herself to take a fresh breath of air, he was gone. Laying back onto the pillow and noting how tossed and turned the blankets were, she got out of bed pulling them into some semblance of order before grabbing her underclothes set out the night before.

Sarah was used to dressing herself although now she was wearing stays again, she needed Lucy to tighten it so Sarah had the narrow waist and high bosoms expected of a woman her age.

Simply thinking of Lucy had that young woman entering the bedroom door with a tray of tea, egg, and toast.

As her friend set the items on the table near the window, she said, "It's a lovely day out and I thought it would be a good day to take a walk, my lady."

"Lucy, you needn't 'my lady' me when it is only the two of us."

"Oh, I thought my lord may be hopping in and out now that he's back." Lucy hurriedly straightened the bedding without mentioning how disrupted it was considering Sarah usually made such a small dent in the mattress and never disturbed the other side of a bed.

"No, the viscount is with the steward, and I am going to do just as I planned unless you think it unwise."

"That's not for me to say, Sarah dear. I was afraid of how this would all work out, but mum and Topher are happy. Toby likes his new position caring for the animals at the home-farm and I, well, I am happy if everyone else is." She stopped neatening up the room and stared at

Sarah. "Is everyone else happy?"

Knowing Lucy would not let it go until she knew that Sarah was fine as well, she finally nodded to her friend. "Yes, I am happy as well. Last night was, um, informational, and I now see the benefits and advantages of marriage between two people who are drawn to one another. I shall never question anyone else's relationship again. I see that it can be extremely—satisfying."

They giggled then laughed blushing merely thinking of what occurs between men and women when others are not around.

"Let me eat this quickly, and we shall go back to the cottage and take Topher for a walk so your mother can rest. As he gets older, I think he is getting to be too much to chase after. We shall need to put our plan into place sooner rather than later, I fear."

"Don't worry about Mum. She's tougher than you think."

Nodding, Sarah finished the cup of tea. "Then I wish to change-out some furniture in the rooms I plan on using most. I also had time to check the nursery and found it well equipped with toys for all ages—even dolls. I shall make sure things that are not safe for little ones will be set aside for now. Topher shall grow into them."

"I hope you get with child soon, and then we can bring Topher here daily. I don't trust that valet. All snooty and had the gall to question my abilities and training after me having trained with the best in London…"

"Now, Lucy, you know the workings of a household like this by now."

"Yes, and it's one reason I had no problems leaving London and coming home to Greater Castleton when you left home. What family cuts off their own kin…"

"Enough of that now, dear. We needn't waste time and energy worrying about the past. We have made new plans, and I think they are better than the first. At least money will not be a worry, and the rest shall work out for the best. Topher cannot be taken from me under the guise I am unable to care for him properly. This has all turned out to be a great relief."

"I know, and I try to concentrate on all the good I see around me. The steward seems interested in doing what's right, and soon there shall only be you and him left to run the place. I only hope…"

"I know. I shall get with child soon and then his lordship shall return to Italy and we shall live our lives as we please. As long as I do not embarrass him, I do not think Lord Wyndom shall have a problem with anything else."

"There you are, pretty as a picture and may I add not looking a day over nineteen," Lucy chuckled as she finished tying the last ribbon holding the back of the morning dress closed.

"Well, I simply wish to appear like the wife of a man owning a home like this. I may meet neighbors if they learn his lordship is in residence. Until then, I plan on working to make this place more to my liking. I may as well be comfortable for it seems I shall live out my life here."

After telling Griffin of her plans, she left him to organize the footmen in placing the furniture into the various rooms. She liked the lighter weight French style for the family rooms and the larger heavier King Charles' pieces to manage Lord Wyndom's large male body in the parlor she thought to use after dinner. They also were more to the man's taste in that they matched the furniture in his sleeping chambers.

Sarah had already gathered the paintings and some items to set on the tables so felt she had time to visit Topher while the men carried the furniture to the rooms she was working on. She would stop by and visit Nanny Wright as well to make sure the old woman was doing well and did not need anything. For some reason, Sarah felt a very close bond to the woman. Possibly because the nurse had known Lord Wyndom when he was small. Knew the man and how he grew to be who he was today.

Sarah approached the Coop's cottage swinging the now empty basket which had held the items she left with Nanny Wright.

A small ball of rags moved and stood tottering on the uneven ground then came toddling toward her with his hands outstretched calling out, "Mine! Mine!"

Bending, she laughed and grabbed Topher's small body before he fell headlong into the dirt trying to reach her. "There is my darling boy."

Sweeping him up into her arms, she nuzzled his neck which still smelled of baby. Soon she knew he would be too heavy for such things, but she would cherish these times for as long as she could.

"Hm-m-m, Christopher Jeffery, how I wish to take you home with me right now and the world be damned." She had to remember not to call him by both names. It sounded too close to his father's which, of course, had been the point of naming him in that manner. At least she had not spelled her son's name the same as his father's. There would still be a way to protect the boy while he grew older. Until a time she could explain what happened and how his father would never have

96

knowingly allowed his son to grow up without a father, without his father's name. That much Sarah was sure of if she doubted everything else about that time in her life now.

She continued to the cottage. Mrs. Coop came out the door and sat heavily into the chair placed next to the whitewashed waddle.

"I expected the sunshine would bring ye over today. The master's been a might grumpy what with those teeth comin' in an all. The little uns don't understand why it hurts 'em."

"The viscount returned yesterday, so I was not able to sneak away without raising plausible questions. I do not think I am ready to answer them so soon. Lucy came home during the middle of the day, did she not?"

"Aye, she did and took the rascal to the home-farm to see the sheep and a late colt who is about to be let out to pasture with the others. Or so Toby explained during supper."

"I bet Topher loved that." Any animal drew her son's attention, and he insisted on touching it as if communing with nature was part of his very being. He was never afraid of them so had to be watched when the plow horse or cattle were out and about. Topher would head directly for them without hesitation often shrieking in glee. The noise, as much as the small scurrying body, sent the animals skittishly shying away.

"I shall take him over to the apple tree and see if there is anything I can reach to glean. He likes the feel of them against his teeth I think."

"Sure to be a few left. I shall send Toby over soon to get the ones still hangin' and make them into something for the boy. Perhaps just fry them up or make them into sauce."

"I shall send some cinnamon home with Lucy from the kitchens. That shall make it even more special for all of you."

"You are a kind girl, um, I mean, thank you, my lady."

Laughing at her son trying to put her hair into his mouth, she pulled it free saying, "Not you, too, Mrs. Coop. I have always been Sarah to you ,so I do not see why that should change."

"Don't you now? Well, I do and it shall be 'my lady' unless I am disturbed with you and then it might be something different." Mrs. Coop showed her less than perfect set of teeth in a cackle and moved slowly into the cottage needing to rest her arthritic knees she earned working in the nurseries and homes of the rich.

****

Tony entered his wife's room by way of the adjoining door to find she was already in her nightgown waiting nervously as she fidgeted with the pleats of the material. Pleased with this arrangement, he moved closer and took her hands in his.

"As beautiful as you appear in this night-rail, I find I prefer us naked in bed together. Less obstacles to get in the way of our enjoying one another, of our joining."

He was not surprised by the deep blush that suffused every portion of her body available to his gaze. Taking the end of the bow tied at the neckline, he gave it a little tug. It came away from its partner loosening the top so that another tug had it sliding down her body, down her arms to the elbows. Yes, the blush was over her entire body, and he thought it charming she still felt shy of him after last night. Perhaps she was shy of the feelings, the desires, he knew welled between them.

"I, ah, I was not sure how you would expect me even after your comments. I was not sure if you would even come to me tonight…"

"The more often we are together as man and wife the more likely you shall get with child."

Licking her lips, she nodded. "And the sooner that happens the sooner you can return to London and the life you have there."

He knew she meant back to Marguerite, but he did not wish to think of the other woman. Not now, not when he was looking forward to bedding this exquisite creature in front of him and not merely for the reason of getting his heir on her so he could then leave her for the months before the birth. For some reason, he felt drawn to Sarah, and their joining was more than the bed-sport he thought it would be, at first. He wished her to enjoy being with him, of course, what man wishes to think he disappointed a bedmate, but this something was more than that.

He felt protective. That was it. He wished to protect this woman from the cruelty she had been dealt in finding love only to have that love forced from her arms to die on a foreign battlefield. Then to be denied his name, their child denied a name because of that first tragedy.

As Sarah stood in front of him with her gown puddled at her feet, he took his time studying the fine bone structure, the rose tipped breasts, the narrow waist which flared invitingly…

Realizing his wife was aware of his slow perusal, he swooped her into his arms and carried her to the bed made ready with the covers pulled down. He kissed her tentatively still unsure of his reception and his world exploded.

Sucking her tongue into his mouth greedily, he felt his member stiffen further although he had thought that impossible. Rubbing his hands over her body, he tried to comfort her with his less aggressive movements, but that only seemed to inflame her more. He broke away from her lips and suckled hungrily at those appetizing nipples, first one and then the other until she breathed raggedly. She stroked his ears as she held his head so he could not leave her if he had tried, and he certainly was not going to leave her now. Not now that his body was aflame with the same kind of desire she was showing.

"Do you like this, my sweet?" he asked as he rose high enough to cover her mouth with his again and rolled the now rigid nipples between his forefingers and thumbs. "Do you wish me to do more?" Their mouths met, and no more was said until they needed time to take a breath.

Her hands continued to hold his head, a finger running around the rim of his ear making him wish to purr like a large mountain cat. One small hand fluttered down his shoulder and over his chest finding a nipple which she circled before moving on to investigate his body more thoroughly than she had ever done.

Holding his breath, he finally felt her hesitate then touch the wiry hair at the base of his rigid erection. She encircled the phallic with her hand causing him to ache with his wish of her.

"Put this in me, please. Fill me with your body." A pleading he did not need to hear as he slid into her easily. Her hips rose to meet him as he plunged into her receding slowly. He did not wish to miss the warmth of her body around him, her body tightening with each penetration as he sought to calm her near frantic thrashings to be closer to him, to reach that pinnacle he had shown her the night before.

Their lips met once again as she held him in place. He lifted her buttocks to take his thrusts until he felt her inner muscles tighten around him, setting off his own orgasm. An orgasm so strong he could not remember having felt the like before. Her enthusiasm for the marriage bed must be the cause. Although he liked and enjoyed this woman, it was Marguerite he loved and wished to be with. This other was simply a happy fluke. A happenstance his wife and he were so compatible and so in tuned with one another physically. Possibly due to the fact they were both younger and such feelings were certainly part of the reason young people mated.

Rolling off her, he laid on his back as she did the same. Panting, catching his breath, and telling himself that this was not being disloyal to Marguerite in any way.

His paramour knew what he had to do. They had discussed it and agreed his marriage bed may be a place where he could be selfish. Where he could be free not to think of being with another woman as being unfaithful to his lover and their relationship. In fact, his getting married to beget an heir had been Marguerite's suggestion. He had nothing to be guilty about, and he had satisfied his wife's need to feel whatever it was she needed.

He did feel he met Sarah's expectation and knew there would be no problems between them for the time he would be part of her life. Only until a child was conceived after which he would be free to live in London as planned with his beloved Marguerite on his arm and in his bed.

****

Sarah walked home after her visit with Topher and recognized the gait of the large man coming toward her with a shovel over his shoulder and whistling.

"Toby, Lucy told me you were liking your job here, but is there anything you think can be done to better the home-farm? I am not sure of the possibilities. Perhaps the storage of fodder or, I don't really know…"

"I do like my job here and I would not wish anyone to think otherwise, Sa, my lady."

"Toby, we are practically family. You may call me Sarah as you always have. It sounds as if you have an idea."

Scratching his head with his cap in one hand, he nodded. "I noticed they still raise Dorset which are fine eatin' for mutton, but the wool's only good for stuffin' or insulation. Maybe bits sittin' next to the chamber pot."

"What are they doing for weaving then?"

"Nothin' that I have on the home-farm. I would think there should be more put into better wool producers so the women could at least make items for their own use. Many places sell the thread even if they don't have their own weavers." He seemed to think a moment before continuing. "I think there should be more fields put into turnips and potatoes, possibly oats. The extras can always be fed to the animals if'n we get too much."

"Those ideas all seem sound to me if there are enough fields readied. And those would all be foods the tenants would wish for their own cellars it would seem."

"Aye, so's I thought, but the rest of the place is right and shipshape. The buildings are whitewashed and the pens clean. Don't have any complaint on how they take care of the animals."

"I shall discuss this with the steward and see what

he thinks, or if there are reasons your ideas cannot be implemented."

Nodding, he slapped his cap back on his head and left Sarah to finish her walk home while contemplating how to approach the steward after their rather awkward start. She had not really spoken to Mr. Fellner since they conversed about the ledgers other than ideas mentioned to him in passing. One being the need for more provisions for the tenants..

Sarah had tried to find funds to cover the shortfall that would occur if they allowed the tenant farmers to keep more of their crops. She had been surprised at how few of the farmers had any of their own livestock knowing that such animals would make a large contribution to a family's winter food.

Later that afternoon, entering the steward's office, she found Mr. Fellner where she knew he would be this time of day. "Mr. Fellner, after speaking with Toby, I really think we should add a better stock of sheep for wool and perhaps milk production. I know cheese is difficult, but we have an old cheese house we can clean and put into use if we have enough sheep providing milk. Perhaps some sort of shared cooperative among the tenants…?"

Glancing up from her notes, her gaze met that of her husband sitting at his leisure in front of the steward's desk. Fellner's face flushed red, and she feared she had interrupted an important conversation. Perhaps they had been discussing just this thing, and here she let it out of the bag that it was her idea rather than the steward's. A man who her husband would have respect and confidence in.

"Oh, I, um, pardon my interruption. It can wait. I

have other things to do…"

Standing, her husband reached toward her and wiped at her cheek with the back of his hand. "Does it have anything to do with the flour on your face?"

Unsure of his thinking about his wife spending time in the kitchens, she tried to improvise somewhat. "I, ah, I was helping make the fruit cakes for the holidays. Cook allows me to putter when I feel the need to be creative."

Now he was smiling, and his eyes seemed friendly and not censorious. "I seem to remember you saying the same about the lace collars and, what were they? Oh, yes, knit booties for the babies being born this winter. Three or were there four due?"

"Four, my lord, but they each need more than one pair."

"Hm-m-m." His gaze pierced hers, and she turned away to find Mr. Fellner watching her now from under his brows. Brows brought low in thought or an attempt not to laugh at how she was going to get out of this without telling the viscount what her plans were.

"I shall let you two gentlemen get on with your meeting. I can talk about this another time."

"No, stay and talk with us now. It seems you have ideas on how this estate should be run, so let me hear it from your own lips." Her husband offered her the other chair which she accepted not knowing what else to do and waited until he took his seat once again.

"As you may have heard, my lord, the tenants shall be having a tough winter since crops were affected by weather this last spring and summer. I have been looking into various means to make up the difference between what they have and what they will need."

Glancing toward Mr. Fellner, she found he had

taken his seat and was listening to her as well.

The viscount turned to his steward and asked, "This is what you meant when you told me about the shortages? That our portion should be less since there had not been as much to begin with?"

"Yes, my lord. The estate has always worked off a percentage, but, as you heard, the crops were hit hard by both too much then too little rain. We also kept too many fields fallow which brought about an even greater shortage."

"And why did we do that? Keep fields fallow?"

Again, the steward's face became red with embarrassment, and Sarah wished she had not chosen that morning to go to the office. At least not without finding out where her husband was first.

"Because, my lord, when I suggested doing so, I was told to keep things just as they had been. It had been working for your father, and you thought the same would continue working."

"I see." Turning to Sarah, the viscount asked, "But you studied the fields in question? Found out about different breeds of sheep, I take it? You wish to diversify more?"

Sarah certainly was not going to let the steward have all of this fall on his head and admitted to her role. "Well, it is safer to do so, my lord. Some sheep do well in certain areas, and some are good for meat and milk. I was merely suggesting we purchase some and distribute them among the tenants to see how they do here. We can still keep what we have and add better wool producers as well as meatier varieties. Some breeds also get larger and mature faster. Both might work well here, and since we have the pasture land, I thought it a good idea."

Nodding, her husband seemed to agree with her. "I do not like to think my tenants and villagers are doing without proper food merely because we have always done things a certain way. I only thought it best not to change anything since it had all seemed to run well under my father's guidance."

His gaze moved to the man behind the desk. "What say you, Fellner? Is my wife correct to think mixing the type of sheep we have is good?"

"It might be time for us to expand, my lord, and investigate the newer breeds. We have always concentrated on a meat breed since we used it here at the estate and sent the rest to the London house, but it is not the best for wool. I must admit that truth."

Smiling, the viscount agreed. "Then we shall invest some of the income this year on buying new stock, and I shall leave it up to the two of you to decide what breed that should be. Possibly try a few of several kinds until we find one that we all agree on." He stood at the end of this speech, and Fellner jumped to his feet as well.

"Coming, my dear?" he asked as he moved to leave the steward now the conversation was at an end.

"Yes, certainly, my lord. I am sure the tenants shall be very happy with your generosity." She glanced at Mr. Fellner but did not allow her gaze to stay on him long. She was pretty sure her husband had more words for her about her easy manner with the steward, and she was trying to find the right words to save her head and the steward his job.

They had barely entered her parlor when the cross-examination began.

"You are becoming quite close with Fellner?" the viscount asked casually, perhaps too casually.

"Close, my lord? I would not say close although we both have an interest in what is best for the estate and the tenants still living here."

"And I do not?"

"If you wish to argue, my lord, then please simply say so. It goes against my nature, but I believe I understand the gist of how it is done."

He laughed and plunked down onto the chair even though she still stood. "I see. I have lost already, have I not?"

"I did not think the argument had begun, but then you know more of such things than I. Do I take a victory lap or some such?"

"No, my dear, but I need to know if you and Fellner have—softer thoughts of one another. Must I worry that my very new, very attractive wife has made a conquest?" His gaze never left her face, and she realized he was very serious with his worry. That he needed her reassurance.

"My lord…Anthony, you have nothing to worry about. I am your wife, and our agreement made everything very clear from the beginning. Your children shall be from your loins, and I shall never do anything to make anyone think otherwise. My love, my heart, is with a soldier left in Spain. I speak with the steward as I do with any other person working in this house. As needed and about what is necessary. As you noted from my arriving straight from the kitchen, I do not consider him a man I am trying to attract."

"I found your dusting of flour quite provocative. I am sure you have been tasting the fruit, and that your lips would prove me correct if I had kissed you back there."

"In the steward's office? What would Mr. Fellner think?" She stared at her husband as if he had gone mad, she was sure.

"I wonder, but it is moot at this point. I still wish to kiss you, but I shall hold myself back so that we do not shock the maids or footmen."

"Now you mock me, my lord. Not well done at all." She smiled seeing that he was teasing and no longer thinking she had eyes on his steward even though he was the second most handsome man in the house.

"No, I do not mock, but I am beginning to realize more about myself. I find I am very possessive, and that is quite unlike me."

"Well, you wish to get me with child and any male you think may be an adversary is apt to get you riled. I hope to have good news for you soon, and then you may return to London and your life there."

"Yes, I am sure you are correct. I should return to London soon either way to visit with my friends. The ones I travelled to Europe with right out of school."

Surprised at this news, she wondered if she would be alone sooner than she thought. "You have not seen them since?"

"I have met up with a few in the evenings or at my club, but never as a group. They planned to come to town and bring their wives..." He glanced away unable to take back the words.

She smiled letting him off any hook he may have thought he bit into. "That should be entertaining for all of you. I am sure their wives are interested in getting to know you as well."

Nodding, he stood saying, "I look forward to sampling those fruitcakes, my dear. Any chance there shall be some tonight at dinner?"

"Minus the brandy, my lord, although I can probably

get Cook to make a brandy sauce to pour over it."

"Sounds excellent, my dear." He left her sitting in her parlor and contemplating what had nearly transpired here today. An argument concerning his worry over her faithfulness while he made arrangements to go to London to stay with his mistress. Sarah wondered how he navigated his two worlds when she had difficulty navigating just her own.

CHAPTER SIX

Sarah and Lucy strolled toward Mrs. Coop's cottage carrying a picnic basket and rug. She spotted her son playing outside the door with Lucy's mother nearby. Topher lost his balance and plopped down on his bottom just as he began shrieking, "Mine! Mine!"

Still laughing at her son, she said, "We have decided to take Topher Jeffery down for a visit to the river. I do not think he will be able to see the fish even if we pointed them out to him, but it shall be a new area for him to discover." She patted his bum saying, "Let's change his cloth and then we shall be on our way. Mrs. Coop, you take this time to rest since he will not be returning until late afternoon. I shall have him nap with us."

"Well, I am bringing my pole. If Toby found out I was by the river and did not at least try to catch him some fish, I'd never hear the end of it," Lucy said, striding into the cottage and returning with a basket creel and rod with bobber. She raised the pole in the air. "Nothing fancy, but it shall get the job done as long as the fish aren't too picky."

Waving goodbye, they began their walk toward the small brook that wandered through the estate coming from the wooded area where the red deer always hid. Sarah had seen them come into the garden foraging for a tasty tidbit in the early morning. She knew the gardener chased them off, but it was pleasant to see the beautiful creatures so close and unaware of her presence.

The stream was cold, but there were fish hiding in the shade of the overhanging bank. Lucy was sure she could lure them into biting the worm she had dug up near a tree trunk.

Topher seemed interested in everything Sarah's friend was doing right up to the worm which he thought he should get to taste before it was put onto the hook. Sarah distracted him by swinging him in her clasped hands while singing a children's song about a robin and a worm.

They dispatched the light luncheon in the basket and chased after Topher keeping him from falling into the water while watching the bobber float downstream.

Topher ran about chasing a small yellow butterfly before toddling over to where Sarah sat on a rug and lay down using her lap as a cushion for his head.

Spying two riders in a distance, Sarah held her breath hoping neither had seen her and the others in the shade of the willow alongside the brook. Not able to warn Lucy without waking Topher, she frantically tried to think of a good story for why she was fishing with her lady's maid and son.

Glancing quickly at the child sleeping peacefully, Sarah tried to slip out from beneath his head and stand to welcome the viscount and the steward as if she did this every day.

"Good afternoon, gentlemen, how lovely this fall day is. We," Sarah indicated Lucy who had laid down her pole and made a quick curtsy when the horsemen rode up to them, "decided it the perfect day for a little fishing. As you can tell, I do not know my way around a fishing rod, but Lucy assured me she did. So far, she has gotten three which I assured her she should take home to her family." Was she talking too much? Was she smiling too widely? She could not tell although both men seemed to be relaxed and content with her explanation.

"A good place to do so as well, my lady," the steward said as he nodded to acknowledge Lucy in his words.

Her husband added, "Possibly we could find a rod and reel for you to try your luck some morning, my lady. I used to know how to get a few nibbles, and Cook always made them taste so good." The viscount was smiling, but his eyes were on the baby waking up and noticing the large horses jangling their harnesses so close to him.

"Mine! Mine!" the little voice said loudly as Sarah closed her eyes and prepared to tell the viscount the whole story and why she had kept her son a secret from him, well, from everyone, besides Lucy and her family.

"Oh, no, little one. These big hooves are not used to missing stepping on someone so small." The viscount chuckled as he backed up his mount. Topher tried to get to his feet and toddle toward the horses now nodding their heads and staring worriedly at the small shrieking person.

"No, Topher, that is not safe, darling." Sarah swooped Topher up and handed him to Lucy who had moved closer to take him from Sarah.

"Here, my lady, let me have him, or he may get your dress dirty with his feet." Lucy lifted the wiggling Topher from Sarah's arms.

Sarah saw what her husband would see. Lucy, blue eyes with her curling blond hair escaping the ribbon she used to tie it back while she fished holding Topher with his tight blond curls laying close to his sweating head and his large blue eyes staring at the man in return. The boy's attention taken off the horses and now focused on the man with the high-top hat.

"Bring him over to pet Major now that I have my mount under control. He will allow you close enough after having time to get used to someone that small." Her husband indicated to Lucy to bring Topher closer.

"Thank you, my lord. He is quite a handful at times," Lucy admitted as she held tightly to the squirming bundle.

"He is a good-looking boy. I am sure your husband is proud of him."

"Um-m, yes, my lord, Toby is right fond of him, he is."

After Topher's little hand petted the horse's neck, he giggled and pulled it back to his chest. The viscount took this moment to pull the horse into moving backward and reined him away turning toward the direction they had come from. "My lady, I shall see you tonight at dinner." He had his fingertips on his hat's brim, and Lucy performed a practiced curtsy even with the extra weight of holding a still wiggling Topher in her arms.

Taking a deep breath, Sarah said, "That was close. I do not wish to have to go through anything like that again." Watching the men ride away, the two women looked at one another with relief.

"But perhaps it's best he saw me and Topher together before he came upon him another time. This way, he thinks I am his mum without either of us having said a word. Even the steward thinks he's mine."

Lucy kissed the baby's head and readjusted how she held him as Sarah folded up the rug they had been sitting on before bending to pick up the fishing gear.

"Probably. It was simply that I thought I could keep my two worlds separate for a while longer. After all, as soon as I am with child, Lord Wyndom shall leave and possibly not return for a couple of years. By then, it will not matter what he thinks or wishes. Topher shall be old enough to understand how to address me and be safe from other people's spite and scorn."

Sarah was determined that her plan work. After all, she had taken a great chance in doing what she had done without telling Anthony her son had lived through the first few months of illness, but by then, Sarah had put about the tale of his passing while Lucy took him to her home where everyone thought she had given birth while away. Toby looking so much like the rest of the Coop family merely gave credence to the story.

****

Sarah saw the door opening before hearing the tentative knock.

"Did you need something, my lord?" Wondering what had brought him to her room before dinner while they both should be dressing, him changing out of his riding clothes and she out of the wrinkled dress she had worn fishing, she watched curiously.

Their gazes met in the mirror. Wearing only her chemise, she still marveled at how easily she could sit there nearly naked and not contemplate grabbing the nearby robe in which to cover herself. His gaze seemed to smolder as he continued to pull his shirt out from the form-fitting riding breeches. His feet were bare, his boots probably already in the hands of his very proficient valet, Harvey, who travelled with him most times.

"When I saw you this afternoon with that babe

sleeping on your lap… I cannot explain the feeling that came over me."

Did he feel the same connection between her and Topher as she did herself? Some unseen bond that kept them tied to one another even when he slept in another house with another family? Was there some look about the boy that she had not detected that screamed she was his mother?

"In what way, my lord?" She prayed this would be something she could handle; some way she could explain her plans that did not sound as if she had been dishonest with him after he had been so honest with her.

The shirt came off over his head and landed on the floor where her gaze followed it unsure as to its meaning. His swift movement began to explain his intentions as he lifted her from the bench she sat on and held her against his now naked chest. Kissing her, he clasped her to him as he pressed her up against the large bedpost taking his fill of her lips.

As usual, his arousal brought on hers. Did every woman have the ability to rouse herself whenever her husband asked it of her? No, demanded it? Without words, he entered this room knowing he would be received, but was that all bad? Was she not only holding up her end of their agreement? That their child would be conceived in passion was simply a bonus was it not?

Working kisses down her body to her breasts while still holding her feet from the floor he muttered, "If we had been alone when I found you today, I would have leaped from my horse and taken you there. Hard and fast without worrying what the world was doing around us. I wished to see you with your own child, our child, in your lap sleeping. Waking to the world with such a wide-eyed curiosity and fearlessness of the horses. A son like that would make a man proud. A woman who could give a man a childlike that so precious."

His words were cut off as he suckled one breast bringing her to a passionate need. Would he always have this capability? Would she wish him to? And if he knew the truth, would he feel the same way?

She felt so humbled that he wished her to bring his seed to life. That he was moved to behaving in such a manner she wished to reward him. Reward him for his passion and his openness about wishing a son—a son from her body. She wrapped her arms around his head and rubbed his ears while putting her leg up around him placing her most intimate part against his hips still clothed in riding breeches.

She did not wish to beg him to take her. After all, it was not as if she was not enjoying everything he was doing, but she wished to feel his body, his hunger inside her. Part of her as they possibly made the son he so much wished. A child that had been only a duty before their marriage   but had now turned into as much of a desire as her husband had become to her. A man who would leave her if he found out the truth. Possibly leave her even before she gave him his heir if he found out about the lie she had told and been living.

She must have whimpered as she felt his passion lessen. She did not wish to lose him but found he was not leaving her as she thought. Instead, he was trying to unbutton his fall and free the engorged erection waiting to spring forth. Pressing herself onto him as he was barely unbound set off a pounding of their bodies until both reached a cataclysmic orgasm. They fell onto the bed, and he rolled to her side with one arm over his head.

Their ragged breathing the only sounds between them.

"Do I need to apologize?" he panted the words out between deep breaths.

"For what?" she managed to pant breathlessly in response.

"For such a display of ungentlemanly behavior. And with my wife, at that."

Turning toward him, she wished to see his expression to gauge how he was feeling. "And who better to behave with such abandon and desire than a wife?"

One eye opened to see her as if he could not believe she had said something so bold. "You are right. Who better?" He sat up and looked about the room seeing her torn chamise and his shirt thrown to the carpet. Leaning over her, he kissed her. "Thank you for understanding. I have nothing to use as an excuse."

"Husband, you need no excuse to come to me at any time. After all, it was not as if we had been down to dinner and passion overwhelmed you during the soup course."

She teased him trying to lessen the guilt he seemed to feel. She was not sure if he felt that guilt due to his interrupting her toilet or if it was because he felt such behavior disloyal to his lady friend in London.

"Now, I am sure Harvey is waiting to dress you for dinner, and I shall return to brushing out my hair of the grass and leaves it picked up this afternoon while rolling about the river banks after a too energetic toddler."

His expression was difficult to read, but the smile he gave her was sincere. Another kiss on her lips and he rose from the bed scooping up his shirt and taking it with him. She giggled to herself wondering what the valet would think about his master disappearing into the lady's sleeping chambers and returning in such a condition. She hoped she had not left marks on her husband's neck where she sucked so passionately trying to get as much of him as she could at the time.

Shaking her head, she picked up the brush and continued to now untangle the mess made from being made love to by a very dear, a very lovable husband.

****

Tony found her in bed, the covers pulled up almost to her chin, but he could tell she lay naked beneath them. Her eyes were open staring at the ceiling which held her interest even as he dropped his robe and slid between the sheets which were warm from her body.

"Do you find me wanton, my lord?"

His brows lowered in concentration as he answered the unusual question. "Do you mean because you anticipated your wedding to your lieutenant? That you bore a child out of wedlock? No, I knew all about that before I approached you."

"I meant about last time. The way I behaved. The way I acted once you began touching me." Her voice quaked as she continued to speak.

He smiled as he pulled her closer to him. "You responded as any husband could wish. I like that you were open with letting me know what pleased you. I was worried about our marriage bed becoming a place I dreaded. That you dreaded."

Should he go on and tell her the worst? He needed to set the basis on as honest a plane as he could. "I feared feeling as if I were raping my wife every time I took you. Your response allowed those fears to vanish and for me to enjoy our time together. I hoped that I would not disappoint, and you helped show me we shall both enjoy this part of our lives together. So, no, I do not find your actions those of a wanton, but those of a very satisfied wife."

"Th-thank you for saying so, my lord. I worried about this all evening and did not wish you to have a distaste of me."

"Just the opposite, my dear. And please call me Anthony or Tony if you shall. I think we are close enough to use one another's Christian names, don't you?" He chuckled and kissed her before she could answer. He did not wish to talk, and he was certain his actions more than his words would make her fears disappear. He felt her relax and accept his touch on her breasts as he began a thorough exploration of her body.

Feeling her hands skim his shoulders up to his head which she held in position as he suckled, he buried all other memories of making love and concentrated on this one woman. This one woman who would become the mother of his children. This one woman who would remain his wife for the rest of their lives. The regret that it was not Marguerite did not hover long as he buried himself into his wife.

Tony entered Sarah's chamber to tell her he would be gone for a couple of days when he saw her sitting at her dressing table crying. He hated to think she was so miserable that she had been keeping her unhappiness a secret from him. This marriage was supposed to relieve her of such feelings, and it tugged at his heart that it had not. Walking over to her, he touched the top of her head making her startle in surprise.

"I am sorry, my lord, did you call for me?" Tear-filled hazel eyes peered up at him and then were lowered as she flushed crimson.

"No, I was merely coming in to tell you something and find you in the doldrums."

"It is that I failed you. I am not with child." Her gaze rose to his face as if waiting for his angry words or signs of disappointment.

"It is too soon to know whether you are or you're not…" Then realizing his error, he stated, "You have begun your courses."

Nodding, she sniffled into her hankie then seemed to bring herself together. Appearing brighter, she said, "It is just that the first time it happened so quickly. I suppose I thought it would always be that way. After all, we have been, um, I mean…"

Chuckling, he patted her shoulder to let her know she did not need to go further in her explanations. "I think we should spend the day together, you know, without the pressure of anything else hanging over us. You mentioned that you rode. Would you accompany me on a ride over the fields today? Get the cobwebs out, as they say."

Her sincere smile was all the answer he needed to know he had said the right thing. He could put off his trip to London and due to Sarah's body, stay longer than he intended once he got there. Marguerite would appreciate his being there over two week-ends he was sure since most important events seemed to occur then.

"Certainly, I merely need to unbury my riding outfit. Do you think the stable master can find a lady's saddle?" She appeared worried she would keep him waiting since he was already dressed for riding.

"My mother had at least one which I am sure Billings has kept in perfect shape. All I need do is change boots and send a note to London."

"Oh, you should not change your plans just to appease me. I am already over my dismals."

"No, there is only a simple musical, and no one shall miss me one way or the other. Another day here will not make that much difference to my plans so shall we say, half an hour?"

"That shall be more than sufficient. I am sure Lucy knows exactly where everything is."

Feeling as if he had taken a burden off his own shoulders rather than helping his wife through a time of melancholy, he turned back to his room calling out for his valet who was already packing for London.

****

The old stablemaster was able to find a horse appropriate for a lady and a saddle which showed many years of care. Her husband helped Sarah into the saddle even though there was a mounting block a few feet away and spread out her skirts before taking the reins to a large black Morgan mix.

He noticed her watching and said, "I find a good-sized horse can take my weight over the fields better than a hunter."

"I thought that might be the reason. That and he is a very handsome mount." She followed him from the stable as they turned in the opposite direction of the village and Mrs. Coop's cottage.

They cantered and soon the territory looked completely different from what she was used to. More trees and less cultivated fields. Many left fallow and barren that year.

"There are many acres in which to ride. Why is it not used for grazing? I see the stone fences are already in place."

Glancing around he shrugged. "I am not certain. I leave that to Fellner since I know nothing about such things."

They slowed their pace even more, and she thought she should explain. "My father was very interested in land use and techniques and would have me read his correspondence to him, even the brochures and published studies on husbandry and farming. I guess I picked up more than I thought. Being out here in the countryside has much of it coming back to me. If you do not think Mr. Fellner shall mind, I would like to ask him about a couple of things."

"You may feel free to ask him anything you wish to know. Remember, he works for both of us now."

Riding side by side was comforting, and she felt closer to her husband than at any time in the marriage bed. He seemed relaxed and allowed himself to enjoy the day.

"Last evening, you said I was 'ready' for you. Can men tell such things? I mean, did I somehow relate to Christopher some sort of signal that I wished what happened? I don't know how it came about so quickly..."

"You have nothing to feel guilty nor ashamed of, especially with me. And I know any man you felt worth marrying was also a man of honor. No matter how much your lieutenant may have regretted not marrying you before he left, he held no regrets about making love to you. You gave him a precious gift any soldier would cherish on the night of his deployment. Do not allow others opinions to tarnish what the two of you had at that moment."

Trying to put the past memories and the subsequent guilt behind her, Sarah nodded, unable to express in words her feelings right then.

Seemingly out of the blue he asked, "Had you no friends who stood by you?"

She understood what he was asking and waited a moment trying to get the right words to explain that time in her life. A time when her family turned against her and only a couple of servants helped her. The same servants she kept separate from her husband at this time.

"I sensed there were, but I did not wish them tarnished by any association with me so I blocked them out. A debutant cannot be too careful with her reputation and shall be painted with the same brush as those she aligns herself with. I even distanced myself from my godmother who has been nothing besides supportive."

"I was merely thinking that now married to me, you could reach out to them. Invite them here to spend time with you. Get to know what is happening with the *ton* so that you have friends when you reenter society."

He seemed as if his words were of no matter to him, but she felt he was merely putting on a show of nonchalance. Did that mean he wished her occupied so that he could return to his paramour? That she would become distracted and not take him to task about getting her with child? Was he tiring of country life and yearning for London and all the gaieties it provided? The ones he had become used to for all those past years?

"My lord, you need not worry about me. I feel well cared for and very content living here as I am. There is no need to keep me company when I know you must have had other plans for this day. Besides, this would be the perfect time to take a week or so in London. Catch up with your own friends and acquaintances."

"Anthony. We are alone together and you should call me Anthony, at least. I shall take that advice since I had made arrangements with my old friends to get together for a game of cards and perhaps a cigar or two. We have been separated since our first year out of school, and I wish to catch up with all of them. The fates aligned this next week for all of us to be in London."

"Then I understand you questioning my lack of friends if you are meeting up with all of them after so many years. So many occasions to celebrate and so many stages to commemorate."

"Yes, that is what I thought, too, when I first thought of setting up this reunion. These men include the ones who traveled with me right out of school. They all returned home at some point along the way. I was the last man unwed and the only one without a child it seems."

The reminder of what she still considered her failure surfaced.

"I am sorry. Perhaps you shall be able to tell them otherwise by the new year."

Glancing her way, he asked, "Ready to shake those doldrums off? I know this next field to be free of holes and such. Should we have a race? I shall give you a head start."

"Certainly, m-Anthony. I think this filly can give you a run for your money."

"Oh-ho, now we have a bet on the outcome?" he asked with a glint in his eyes.

"Well, since I have no money, but what belongs to you already, I shall think the winner shall name the prize."

He tipped his head saying, "I accept."

The word had barely left his lips when she urged the little mare into leaping into a full gallop. Sarah laughed with the exhilaration of the ride even though she knew it was a fruitless effort to try to beat the black her husband was riding. It soon passed her, and all she saw was the wind through the animal's long mane and feathered fetlocks. She wondered what kind of a forfeit Anthony would ask of her. Chills went up her spine thinking of the possibilities.

*****

They were walking the horses at a slow pace to allow them to cool down.

Sarah asked, "Do you remember your childhood here in the country? Did you have playmates, or were you sent away to school early? And do you wish the same for your son?"

By being so persistent not to allow one side of his life to interfere or cross over into the other, Tony seemed to have made himself a complete mystery. Not that there was anything mysterious about himself, he had a rather predictable younger life and then a rather unpredictable twenties—now leading into his stable thirties. Stable in the sense he was a married man trying to beget a family and appearing to hold a normal Englishman's lifestyle. The life he lived in Italy with Marguerite was as different to this one in Wyngate as he could imagine.

He began where he felt his life began. As he realized there was more than Wyngate and those attached to it.

"I was raised here in Wyngate until they sent me to school at Eaton. Nanny Wright watched over me while my parents spent most of their time in London or Bath depending on the time of year. I saw them when they passed close enough to make it easier to stay here than anywhere else, but I cannot say I missed them. They were my parents, and I wrote to them monthly, just as Nanny instructed, until going off to school where it seemed more time passed between letters."

"That sounds lonely to me. I was raised and mostly schooled by my parents. My mother did a good job teaching me the needed domestic skills, and my father thought it best for me to understand how life worked— especially agriculture. He thought the world revolved around farming, and in a way, he was correct. If agriculture fails then so shall the entire system including government. Look what happened when the French peasants went without bread."

"Interesting ideas—especially to pass down to a female child."

"You do not think children should be taught about the world as a whole and not just the little snippets that touch their life?"

"No, probably just the opposite. If my travels taught me one thing it was that every man thinks he knows what is best and how to go about making the world better while ignoring others. Each country works toward its own best interest which many times is not best for others. The ones who seem to work are the ones, like England, that colonize and then alter the existing society. I am not sure that is the correct manner of going about doing such things and stating such ideas aloud probably amounts to treason."

"Perhaps, but many men have such discussions about such things all the time if my father's correspondence is anything to go on. Some for colonization and some against, some wishing one large universal country all working together for the betterment of mankind. No one taking more than they need while sharing with those unable to provide for themselves."

"Now that sounds treasonous…" He smiled taking the sting out of the words. "And what are your ideas?"

She seemed surprised he would ask. As if no one had actually ever cared enough to inquire before. "I believe all children should have an education so as to be able to form their own opinions. They should be free to work where they wish rather than where they were born, and that anyone can alter their circumstances with hard work and ingenuity. That who their father was or was not is not something that dictates their entire life."

He thought she had some very definite ideas on life and how things should go on. He thought they seemed agreeable and noted her emphatic need that a child's destiny not be based on its father or rather, even having one. He could see where her entire life was now saddled with one mistake in judgement she had made as a young girl. How that stigma had dictated the limited choices she had for her future.

Seeing the edge of the forest, his horse sped up spontaneously.

"There is a tree fort I used to visit. Jamieson, the gamekeeper at the time, accompanied me when I traveled this far from the main house. He fished in the brook running through just over there while I played all sorts of fantasies of my own making."

Turning to him, her smile was so lovely he felt compelled to tell her his most embarrassing truths.

"Such as?"

"Oh, slaying the dragon and rescuing the princess, killing the troll and standing tall on the top of the bridge. Things like that. Probably ideas gotten from those ridiculous fairy tales Nanny used to read to me from the books in the nursery."

As he pulled his horse to a halt under a tree naked of leaves, Tony dismounted and took her reins to tether her horse next to his. Then putting his hands on her waist, lowered her to the ground. He was not sure what emotion ran though his body like the blood he needed for life, but there was something. Something that made him stand close to her long enough to inhale her scent. Long enough to raise interest in another part of him as he turned away.

"If it is still standing, the fort should be through here in a small clearing."

The clearing was gone, but some of the stout boards he had used as the floor of his towering fortress were still present. Other places rusted nails showed where the half walls had once been nailed to the gnarled branches of long ago. More than twenty years had passed, and this tree, just as his life, had changed in innumerable ways.

They spent an hour finding the areas Tony remembered from his youth. The bank where the Keep fished and napped, the special stone half-buried in the dirt that Tony had used as the stone from which to pull his wooden sword, the path into the woods which was mostly grown over. Probably once a deer path, it seemed abandoned and lost among the leaves now.

Each find opened memories of his childhood and the estate in general. Remembering it was Billings who carved the sword for him and a groomsman who put together a leather scabbard for it. Nanny's reminder of certain stories or heroes she thought he would like to pretend to be was one of the last things she told him whenever he left to go to the woods. It was one place she never accompanied him by saying she was not equipped for such an adventure.

Telling his wife these stories now made him wish to see his own sons doing the same things as Tony did only instead of the games-keeper they would be there with their father. He would help them rebuild the tree fort. He would show them the secret magical rock. He would tell them the stories of King Arthur or how to slay the dragon and save the princess.

But how could he think to do these things while living in Italy? Living in a country that would take him weeks to return from if anything should befall one of his children. How was he to be the father he wished he had had and honor the promises he made to Marguerite? He did not wish these thoughts tainting his day remembering his childhood which now seemed idyllic. How was he to be both a good father and a good paramour?

CHAPTER SEVEN

"I wish you did not need to return to the country. Why could not you rent a town house here in London for her to stay in until she is *enceinte*?"

Tony came up behind Marguerite wrapping his arms around her and pulling her so she leaned against him.

"Because then people would expect me to show up to events with her on my arm. I mean a newlywed does not leave his bride at home alone. Not until she is with child. By the time the babe, is born, it shall seem normal for the two of us to be a couple."

Turning in his arms Marguerite pouted up at him. "But it is not the same when you are away. Most of the invitations that arrive are for you. No one ever mentions me, and I think I am only welcomed on sufferance when I am with you. It is you they seem to wish to see."

"Well, it has been years since I was back, as you know, and there are those who knew me when I was still in school. Since I became Wyndom, there are those who wish to get to know me for various reasons. I may not have a seat in the House of Lords, but my lands and wealth allow me to have a voice."

"But that leaves me—where?"

This had been an on-going argument between them for the past few days, and Tony had run out of patience trying to convince Marguerite he wished to be with her, but he also needed to beget an heir.

Her whining continued. "On the Continent, in Italy, I was someone. I was a *contessa* and was sought as a person of consequence. Everyone included me if they wished to be known as a popular hostess, but here, here I am a widow waiting for my *innamoroto* to reappear and escort me to the places he has been invited."

"That is not so, and you know it. You are the most attractive and witty of party guests. You can have any man you wish, and I am so thankful you wish that man to be me. You still stir my heart as no other, and if I spend time in the country, you know it is to get my heir so I can then spend time here with you."

He used his best cajoling voice to woo Marguerite into a better mood. He knew this plan would be difficult on her even if she had agreed it was the only way for him to get his required heir and for them to remain together. Not many debutants or their mothers would have allowed him to parade a mistress around so soon after the wedding. Sarah's lack of parental care had helped him decide she would be perfect for his plan.

"Come, we shall go out this evening, and we shall attend at least three events and not return home until the early hours of the morning."

Fanning her lashes at him seductively, she said breathlessly, "Not too early in the morning. I miss our private time together as well. I know my body is not as young and firm as you are used to, but..."

"None of that kind of talk." He kissed her mouth then looked down at her noting the fine lines about her petulantly pouting lips, and said, "We promised one another in the beginning there would be no such comparisons. I keep the two lives I live separate from one another, and it shall remain so. I cannot compare the years of loving and life we have spent together with the brief time I have been married. The time we spent with one another forged the bond that keeps us as one. Now, let us find our capes, and we shall begin our evening setting London on fire."

Smiling, she nodded, the feather in her hair bouncing with each movement. A wave of guilt washed through him as he looked at her and pictured Sarah dressed in such a fine dress and jewels. Perhaps he should bring his wife back a present. After all, he had not given her a bride gift with all the haste of their marriage. He should find time tomorrow to stop in to one of the jewelry shops on Bond Street before going to lunch at his club.

Bouncing along in the enclosed carriage, Tony felt a sense of excitement which he tried not to analyze. He had just spent over a week with the woman he loved so why was his body feeling an awakening? As if it had been waiting for this time, this trip back to Wyngate and the life waiting for him there? The quiet life focused on begetting his heir and then leaving the place in his wife's capable hands?

And he did think they were capable. The missives his steward sent him were different than the ones sent before and arrived more often. Fellner usually reported quarterly, but recently there had been all sorts of questions and the steward needing permission to spend monies on buying new stock and changing crops. These things were never discussed before. In fact, Tony assumed the man did as he pleased and as long as the outcome was acceptable, Tony had never questioned the man's choices.

He was sure his wife had something to do with the

many notes and questions. After all, he could see she had taken an interest in the place from all the changes he saw being made. Not only the change in furniture, but the change in his staff—their attitude at least. They used to walk around him when he visited as if on eggshells, but now they welcome him each morning when he arrives downstairs and are eager to make sure he is comfortable. Griffin had even made a personal comment on how much he and the staff appreciated the new viscountess' attention to details. How happy Griffin and his wife were to have someone care about the house and grounds again.

The comment had made Tony think about his mother and the fact the woman had never shown love or care about the country place. She had stopped off there infrequently and only if they were in the neighborhood. Even when he was home from school, his parents were often absent. Nanny Wright and Billings in the stables had made up his family during those school years the same as they had before he went away to school.

In later years, his parents could usually be found in London although his father did pay attention to the estate and its needs. Not that he seemed all that keen as a farmer, but the man did appreciate his duties and made sure there would be no blame left on his shoulders when he passed on the title and lands.

Well, Tony was not his father, and if Sarah wished to try her hand at animal husbandry and land management, then she could have at it. If it meant she was content to stay in the background, maintain his home, and raise his children, then he was going to support her—at least until the steward told him she was driving the place to rack and ruin. Then he might try to curtail her efforts, but so far, Fellner seemed to agree with her, so Tony could leave things be.

Besides, it was not as if Tony would be spending much time at Wyngate. Not after he had gotten Sarah with child. He would have concluded his business and could do as he wished—at least until the child was born. Tony still had not decided how to go on after that event. Before they left Italy, he thought they would return to the sunny clime, but now, after being back in England and seeing some of his old friends living there happily, he had begun to think he may need to stay. Stay and visit the child as he grew. If it was not a son then he would need to get another child upon his wife and try again as soon as was practical.

Thinking about staying on in England reminded him of the past week and the whirlwind of events Marguerite thought essential to be happy. They barely had time to sleep. She had filled their social calendar so full. Morning breakfasts that lasted half a day followed by afternoon shopping or rides in the park when blessed with nice weather. Evenings began with dinner at one home, a musical or dance at another, a ball and then cards and gambling. He was glad he had brought Harvey since his clothing was getting a work-out and his dance shoes worn out.

But at least Marguerite seemed happier than when he arrived. That was until it was time for him to leave today. He had been gone from Wyngate well over the week he thought he would be gone. Each time he mentioned returning, Marguerite found another invitation she had accepted for the two of them, and of course, it was too late to cancel. He finally had to tell her he was leaving, and that she would have to attend alone or ask another escort.

Pouting was not pretty on a woman her age, but he restrained himself from saying so. He knew she was a woman who enjoyed the bright lights and music and the admiration of others whether it was women envious of her jewels and gowns or men who coveted what the Viscount Wyndom had. It had cost him a trip to the jewelers on Piccadilly Street, but he got out of London in a halfway decent time. He would be home late, possibly missing his dinner, but not too late that he could not visit his wife.

Mere thoughts of such a visit made his male member react. Crossing one leg over the other brought himself under control. After all, he did not wish to waste an erection when he was still hours from home. Hours from the woman he would be bedding that night. The woman he hoped would welcome him as she had for the first ten days of their married life. Thinking of her made him smile as he had not since leaving her.

He wondered what she had spent her time doing besides changing every piece of furniture in the main rooms. Or making soup and bread with Cook to take to the shut-ins and new mothers on the estate. Or making lace collars and booties, whatever those were. Or bothering his steward about a new grain or crop to plant next spring.

Thinking about that, he wondered when he had picked up so much knowledge of what she did to keep herself occupied. When had he taken the time? Why had he bothered since he was leaving her and the estate as soon as she got with child? He did not find the knowledge concerning, but perhaps there would be more between him and his wife than merely a child, his heir. Perhaps he should be thinking about all those same things as well. Become the viscount worthy of his viscountess.

Tony hurried to his sleeping chamber after sending his valet to his own rooms. Tony felt he could undress for bed without aid. In fact, he had been thinking of nothing besides undressing and making love to his wife for the past mile.

Sarah was already in bed, her glorious hair shining gold and red in the candle's light as it flickered on its stand. He felt younger, lighter merely being in this room with her. He grinned in relief before other thoughts took over his mind and body.

"I wish to kiss you all over. I wish to taste every part of you from your lips to your toes," he whispered as he moved toward her.

Giggling, she nestled into the sheet and waited as he dropped his robe to the floor and climbed in beside her. "You think I tease, but I have a ravenous hunger for you that may take hours to satisfy."

He realized this was not simply love talk, but how he truly felt. When had he become so honest with a woman in bed? When had his other sexual intimacy become merely a formality? A timed occurrence almost to a set regime? He threw out such thoughts as he always did in this bed and covered Sarah's mouth with his own. He drew from her the desired response of her passion for him. Her natural desire for his body and what he promised to do to hers.

After a heated interlude, he rolled to his side with barely enough breath to whisper, "If that does not make a baby then nothing I ever do shall."

Her smile was half hidden beneath her unbound hair. "I see you returned well motivated. I take it you wish to be done with needing to stay in the country week after week? That you find London much more to your liking?"

"No, not more motivated than I was. In fact, I find I enjoy having the simpler, quieter way of life to escape to."

Teasing, she chuckled. "Do not tell Cook that. She is sure having your favorite dessert of lemon trifle was what motivated you to hurry home in the dark of night."

"Hm-m-m, it does have its attractions, but I am not sure it competes with this other. Perhaps there is a way to combine the two? Tell Cook to serve the lemon trifle again tomorrow night, and I shall see if my plan works."

****

Waiting naked in bed, the candle light flickered as the door to the adjacent chamber opened, and her husband glided through. He wore just a robe and carried an unfamiliar article.

Sarah was intrigued. "What have you brought?"

"Oh, this? Merely some of Cook's trifle in case I felt a little peckish during the night."

Thinking this was an unusual thing for him to do, Sarah nestled lower in the bed as he set the dish on the table next to the bed by the candle. Shrugging out of his robe, his skin glistened in the firelight just long enough to become interesting before sliding between the sheets next to her. She was amazed at how his eyes glittered with humor and his dimples framed a grin that reminded her of what he must have looked like as a schoolboy planning on getting into trouble after lights out.

Not waiting before covering her mouth with his, she smiled tasting the lemony fruit taste on his tongue. "You have been sampling already. I thought you said you would share?"

"Oh, I plan on sharing." He dipped a forefinger across the frothy topping, and she began closing her eyes and opening her mouth for the tasty treat she knew it would be. Startled, her eyes popped open as the sticky dessert was swiped across one budding nipple leaving a coolness followed by the warmth of his mouth. He sucked the lobe as far into his mouth as possible.

She was happily content at how satisfying his suckling from her breast felt and how she hoped this game between them would continue. Sharing a dessert took on a completely carnal version as he dipped and spread then licked several heretofore uninitiated body parts.

Seemingly too full to contemplate another sampling, he leaned back smiling at what his ministrations had done to her self-control as her body flushed with desire and nipples quivered with anticipation.

Placing a finger full of trifle on one of his nipples, she leaned over him to lick the creamy concoction making sure to clean the hair roughened area surrounding the now glistening nub. When she was satisfied with her exertions, he exhaled and lay supine beside her.

Taking another fingertip full, she placed a dollop on his engorged manhood then stared at his trembling reaction and glanced furtively to his face. His eyelids were almost closed, but she could see the glitter of his eyes as he watched her through thick lashes.

"Was that too bold?" she asked hesitantly, unsure of herself and questioning her instincts.

Breathlessly he said, "Nothing is too bold between us in this bed."

Satisfied she had not offended him in any way, she

bent to lick delicately so as not to harm the velvety soft crown of his phallic erection. She saw the muscles tighten across his stomach and heard his whisper plea, "Sarah, you are killing me…"

Taking that to mean she should finish his absolutions she sucked in the top to make sure she left him free of the sugary mixture. She felt his hands grasp both sides of her head to hold her in place. She finished licking him thoroughly when he growled, rolling onto her.

"Enough! I think we need to finish this now before I do something I had not planned."

Pressing into her with a harsh release of air he muttered, "I have never wished you so much…wished anyone so fiercely."

His thrusts, though fast and furious, drove her to her climax just ahead of his own and left them panting entwined in a pile of now relaxed body parts.

Sarah recovered before he did and curled into him, saying, "I like eating dessert in bed with you. Do you think syllabub would have the same effect?"

His guttural groan and an arm snaking out to pull her closer was his only response.

****

When had he and Marguerite stopped being as free and giving in bed? The first few years he remembered as being gloriously uninhibited. Unable to get enough of one another or at least he could not get enough of Marguerite. Then, he remembered it was upon a return trip to Italy after running into old friends in Prussia. Something changed during the middle of a weekend at a country castle. Tony had been out hunting and upon his return he realized Marguerite was not her same laughing bubbly self. She pretended to be all right, but he could tell something had happened which she refused to discuss.

He thought once they were back to sunny Italy, she would return to her pleasant entertaining self, but it never quite happened. Instead, she went to wearing wigs more often and more powder. He even thought she was blackening her brows, but was not going to comment upon it. She was lovely no matter what she did.

But that was when they began sleeping in separate beds, separate rooms more often. Before that, he had spent his nights in her bed, but after that weekend, she told him she would rather not share a room. That she could sleep sounder if he left her and returned after her maid was finished dressing her in the morning. It was also the same time she began wearing nightwear to bed. Before that, they had slept naked together without that diaphanous material getting caught-up between them all the time.

It was the same time making love was consigned to the evening hours and candles were dispensed with. No light could cast its glow across the bed or reveal their entwined bodies. Not that such light was necessary for a thoroughly satisfying outcome, but it was one more indication Marguerite felt less than comfortable around him. That she felt lacking in some way, and he had no idea how to convince her otherwise. That he found her as desirable, as exciting as he ever had.

Tony wished to tell her he did not care about the wigs. That he had seen her without them, and the gray strands in her hair had no effect upon his love for her. His desire for her, but then he decided if it bothered her so much to have him see her in less than perfect dress and toilet, he would accept relegation to his own room. A woman has her vanity, and he would accept that Marguerite felt she was getting older, but then so was he. Did she not add that into the equation? Or was that part of it? Did she not find him as attractive and wished for the space between them so she could find comfort alone? Without having to see what time was doing to them both?

The argument that finished his last visit to London concerning his finding a wife once he calmed Marguerite was not one he wished to remember. Still, he thought the question had been settled. Now less than a week since he had spent more time than he should in London, another summons appeared on the salver Griffin brought to him at breakfast.

Memories of a similar missive invaded his mind. After Marguerite had agreed to his plan of begetting an heir without the time-consuming problem of finding a proper wife who would be acceptable for his need to have a lover within walking distance of his townhome, his paramour, once again, fell apart. He had been summoned to London within moments of arriving at Wyngate with his new bride. Instead of the wedding night he thought he would have, he raced back thinking something dire had befallen his lover. Instead, he found Marguerite in distress over seeing his bride in the church where he had told Marguerite not to be.

Realizing she was simply showing her immaturity and control over him, he refused to be used as her martinet. Once he found she was not ill or in need of anything, he spoke seriously with her about his wish to stay beside his bride for at least the first month. He would return to London to escort Marguerite whenever he could, but she should plan to attend functions without him or to take one of her male friends which she seemed to accumulate no matter where she went.

Marguerite had not been happy but said she understood the need to get his wife with child so the rest of their plan could be put forward. He was hoping this note calling him to return to London was not of the same ilk. He also hoped that she was not seriously in need of him in some other way, either. Thinking of her laying ill or injured, needing his strength or support made him wish the carriage could travel faster over the frost covered roads.

But worrying would not solve his dilemma. He would know what the problem was when he reached her side. The note said to go to her home, that he was needed and that was what he would do—once again.

He raced up the stairs to her room only to be confronted by a lovely Marguerite dressing for the day.

"Are you telling me you sent that message so that I would come to London to take you driving in the park?"

He stared at the woman he had been worrying about for the past few hours. Ever since he left the warmth of his country home to race across dangerously compromised roads. Hours of thinking what may have befallen her or why the note had not said more except to go to her home rather than his own when he arrived. The wording indicated she was not well enough to leave her own home. He could only stare at her now in amazement that she felt no compunction as to calling him back to London for such a trivial thing.

"A lady does not ride in the park alone, and I have so few friends here. Of course, I thought you would be pleased to spend a few days in town. Besides, I have this lovely *chapeau* I had made specially for me."

She tweaked the curls showing at the side of the hat he thought too frilly for a woman Marguerite's age. It appeared as something a debutant looking for attention would wear.

"I had it designed after seeing one similar on Lady Suzanna's head."

Smiling, he said words about how lovely she looked but knew Lady Suzanna was a young woman half Marguerite's age and not known for her fashion sense in the least. His mistress had always been considered a leader of fashion in Italy so what had happened to her otherwise good taste? He was missing something, but he had to worry about getting back to Wyngate to keep up his attempt at fathering the next viscount.

"I do not think that would be a good idea, darling. Why don't we plan on going out to dinner and then on to whatever event is being held? I promise to dance with you at least twice and pay all my attention to you." He smiled hoping she would not prove difficult and stomp her tiny foot demanding to be driven to the park.

"But I shall not be able to wear my new bonnet. You must have time since you were not even planning on being here in town." She pouted and placed her hands on his shoulders with a pleading expression.

Hating the idea of being confined in a carriage and jostled over the roads again already, he conceded, hoping to appease her into a good enough mood he could trust her not to make a scene once she was in public.

"All right, I shall take you for a drive, but not through the park at the busiest time of the day. I shall take a drive out to Richmond Park."

"What is this Richmond Park?"

"It is a lovely place, I assure you, and there are races

held there in the better weather. You shall enjoy the drive." He carefully chose his words without telling her it was an hour trip one way and out of town to the countryside rather than the center of prestigious London as Hyde Park was.

"I can be ready immediately." She pranced cheerfully to collect her lace gloves.

"Fine, we shall lunch at a little inn I know." He watched as she went to get her outerwear and thanked his lucky star Marguerite was not familiar with London's geography. He gritted his back teeth knowing this whole trip had been a ruse to get his attention back on her. He had hoped she would accept the time he needed with his wife to ensure there was a child on the way, but found himself once again in town and missing the opportunity to be with his young wife. Something he found he missed more than he would have thought.

As he feared, the trip to Richmond was not filled with the *ton* Marguerite wished to impress. As they traveled, he realized his lady-love was not attracting the attention she always craved and received on the continent. The Italian aristocracy was not as popular as the French *émigré* flooding London. The latter had better stories and usually closer relationships to many aristocrats and the *contessa* had not any ties to England other than himself.

Once they were back in her townhouse, Tony tried to explain, once again, why he needed to return to Wyngate. He must have shown some of his displeasure at her constant demand for his time.

"This would be different if I were able to give you your heir. With you I would have gladly lost my figure and look like a cow for months on end."

"I do not think I understand what you are saying, Marguerite. I understood you had conceived once, but lost the baby and your ability to bear a child at the same time."

He watched her turn from him before explaining, "It was not the same thing. I would have gladly had your child if we had met first. If it had not been for marrying such an old man." She pouted and tossed down her gloves.

"But your husband, the count, was only forty-four when he died. That is not much older than..." He thought better of finishing that statement by reminding her she was over forty and did not think of herself as old.

"And I was, but nineteen to his forty-four. It is different for a woman. He was soft and gray and wrinkled in places that were most distasteful. He already had three children with his mistress who had as nice a home as he provided me with. I was useful to him, and he took advantage of my father's need for money. I was sold like some cow or mare to a man my father's age."

"Darling, I know all this, and I agree you had been treated shabbily, but that was years ago. Why do you keep bringing it up?"

"Because now there is reason for me to regret what I did back then..."

"What are you talking about? Losing the baby? You had no hand in that. These things happen, and I understood when we first became interested in one another. You told me you were barren due to a problem you had with your first pregnancy. I accepted that we would never have a child together back then. Telling me you also never wished to remarry was more difficult to accept, but I did with time. The money you received from your husband's estate gives you the independence you crave. You are not dependent on anyone although I would never leave you."

"Anything could have happened, and since there was no reason for us to marry then, why should we have tied one another down? Besides, we were happy the way things were, but now I have misgivings. If I could have foreseen the future, I may have done things differently."

"In what way? I do not understand." Holding her hands, he tried to comprehend her new concerns. Her words did not make sense to him. All this was in the past and none of it her fault.

"It, um, was not losing the infant that made me infertile. That was caused by the infection after the procedure. The woman who saw to me never said it would cause permanent damage. I merely did not wish to have a child so soon. I knew the *conte* would send me to his country estate once I was with child, and then he would forget about me. I was too young to be buried in the country." Tears rolled down her cheek. Tony did not think any of them were for the child she lost, but for herself. Her own feelings of being neglected and overlooked by a man old enough to be her father.

"Marguerite, explain this to me. It sounds as if you did something to end your child's life so that you could remain in society. Continue to live the social life of a *contessa*."

She seemed unable to look at him while she said the words. "I was young and did not fully realize what it would mean not to be able to provide my husband with a child. He sent me to the country to recover and then rarely sent for me to attend anything as his wife. He even cut my pin-money in half saying I did not need as many gowns since I was destined to live in the country. His mistress began to accompany him everywhere, and I think many forgot he had a young wife wilting in the country."

Unsure if he understood her motivations as well as she did, he said, "A wife who denied him his chance of an heir so she could continue going to parties and buying pretty things."

"It was not like that. Anthony. You do not understand." She balled the hankie up in one fist turning from him, refusing to even attempt to look him in the eye any longer.

"Then help me. Help me understand how a woman could rid herself of her own child? I agree I am a man and it is different for us, but to end all possibility of a having a child?"

Whispering she admitted, "I was, but a foolish child. Children should not be wed to men who demand so much from them. I was not ready to be a mother for any man's child. I never thought it would make me barren. I knew that at some point I would have to bear my husband's children, but just not then, not so soon after getting the independence of a married woman. Of tasting society and all the shops and balls and parties. Of being flirted with by other men who said I was beautiful and charming and all that was good in the world." She peeked up at him and quickly added, "I was very immature and did not understand the possibilities."

"But years later when we met, you told me a completely different story. You seemed upset that you never had children." He remembered the day she shared her secret as if it pained her to tell him these things.

"Perhaps I was then, but what did it matter? The

chance to be a mother was long past for me and for you…you said it did not matter." Waving into the air, she added, "And now look at how much you have changed your life to make it happen."

He had to agree. When he was younger, Marguerite being barren was not even cause for him to blink let alone think of the future. The future had seemed so far away. His father was healthy, and the money was flowing into his bank each quarter so why did he need worry about an heir or a wife, for that matter. It was only in the face of being the last in his line that made him realize his duty. To provide the title and the estates with someone to care for it and all those who depended on its healthy continuance.

Handing her his clean dry handkerchief, she used it to wipe her face. The powder and light rouge removed with them left her looking aged and sad. What was he doing? The woman he thought he loved turned out to be someone he never knew. He thought all these years they were loving and living a life that had been dealt them. Both acting as a married couple yet knowing there would never be a true reason for them to marry. While he had tied a young woman with other options to living and birthing the children this woman was unable to.

His sense of honor had taken a beating these last few moments. Not only had he been deceived for years by a woman he had pitied for the difficult life she led, he had dragged another into the mire. He had much to think about on the trip home.

Entering Whites, Tony felt he had been gone a lifetime rather than the few weeks of his time at Wyngate.

"Tony! Tony, how good to catch you here. Have you

had luncheon yet?

"No. I thought to drink my lunch." After leaving Marguerite last evening right after the bombshell she had dropped on him, he had stayed awake most of the night questioning everything he thought he knew about their relationship. About why and how they had spent their time together. As he looked back, he felt it all a lie, a waste.

His friend James Everett laughed pushing him toward the table James had just vacated. "Like that is it already, old son? I thought once you finally settled, you would have chosen the perfect mate for yourself."

"No, it is not due to my wife. So far, I have not any complaints in that quarter. She has taken to being my viscountess easily and without reservations."

His friend's brows rose almost to his hairline as he said, "Lucky you. Perhaps waiting was the correct thing to do, but my mother would have none of it. Besides, Babs is a fairly good sort and gives me a long leash, but I know there is a leash so that may be the rub."

"My sympathies, old friend, but I have seen your wife and many men would not mind being on a leash if a woman as lovely as your wife were at the other end."

Tony laughed as he got the attention of one of the waiters and mimed needing a drink. He relaxed as the man seemed to jump and hurry toward the sideboard where the bottles were kept.

"You are right, of course. I do not feel the leash like I did when I was first married. With a wife such as Babs, who needs his freedom to chase after actresses and doxies?" He glanced toward his friend before daring a personal comment. "You still have that Italian *contessa*? I am not sure I would waste time on her with a new wife at home."

"Enough, James. I do not allow anyone to discuss my friends and the *contessa* is my friend."

James took his glass in hand and peered into it as if to find the truth. "I thought she was more than that."

"She is, but I do not talk about how close of a friend. I think it best for both women involved, and I do not wish to hurt either one of them with unneeded speculation if you do not mind."

"No, I understand. Life can be a bit confusing. I am just happy that you have finally made your way back home. We all plan on getting together with the wives during the holiday season. You and your wife are expected, of course. Suffolk's home with everyone, even children are invited."

"I shall have to get back with you on that. Lady Wyndom does not care for London or society very much and prefers the country."

"Is not that what I just explained? We shall be at Suffolk's country estate with all the frills and gewgaws. Babs and I are staying up till Christmas with the boys who are home from school. You have never met them before, and I would like for you to do so before they reach their majority."

James chuckled while Tony tried to do the quick math and realized how long he had been from England. Comparing what the rest of his friends' lives had become with his own. One was worried about the come out of his oldest daughter which his wife was already planning.

Raising one brow, Tony looked to his friend. "I do not think it shall take me that long to make my calls, but I still shall need to get back with you on that."

"Really? You let your wife dictate…oh, wait, are

you trying to tell me that you already have a start on your nursery? Babs' first few months weren't fun at all. She got all sort of food yearnings and then tossing up her accounts…" He became quiet then added, "No, I think the sickness came first followed by the food yearnings. Yes, I am sure that is how it went. Been a while, don't you know, so one forgets such things."

"As far as I know, my nursery is as empty as it has always been." Tony felt he should give some warning so it was not a complete shock to his friends. "Of course, such things do happen, and it is not as if I spend all my time here in London…"

James peered at him then shrugged. "I know what people are saying, and the woman herself has not done anything to keep them from talking. The *contessa* makes it known wherever she goes she is still a very close friend of Lord Wyndom and hostesses should keep a seat at the table for you since you visit her regularly."

Tony bit back a rude remark, but it was not James' fault if Marguerite still felt the need to use his name as entry to London society. He was not used to his paramour finding the need for such things, but then Marguerite probably felt out place and needed his influence behind her. His name to keep her from being thought of as a second-tier guest.

"How are the others? It sounds as if you have seen each of them since I have?"

Tony motioned the waiter over to place their meal order while James proceeded to list where and when he had seen their mutual friends.

CHAPTER EIGHT

Striding into Sarah's bed chamber, Anthony shrugged out of his robe leaving it draped over a chair while continuing to walk toward her with his magnificent erection jutting proudly from its nest of curly dark hair.

"You are a truly handsome man." The honesty blurted from Sarah's mouth, but his smile rewarded her unguarded tongue. She opened the covers showing him she lay naked waiting for him. "I was not sure you would come to me tonight. Not after your late arrival home."

"Yet, here you are seemingly eager for our coupling."

His hand met hers, and their fingers laced with one another's as if they had been doing this for years instead of mere days.

She glanced at their joined hands. "Your hands are strong yet so gentle with me. Neat and clean."

Chuckling, he replied, "Harvey becomes despondent if I even chip a nail. He is responsible for the filing and buffing of them so perhaps he should receive these compliments."

Sarah could see she had embarrassed him. Evidently, he was not used to hearing his many attributes listed, but tonight she wished to repay him for her life here. If she could not confirm a pregnancy, at least she could tell him how beautifully attractive he was. Freeing one hand from his, she rubbed the rim of his ear.

"You have exquisite ears, and I quite like kissing and licking them."

If she had not been watching his face so closely, she would have missed the increase of color to his skin. A blush? Her rugged, debonair husband could blush?

"And then there are your broad shoulders which I also like to kiss although I do apologize for getting carried away in moments and leaving your body marked."

"Love kisses," he whispered, kissing the inside of her wrist on the hand still petting his ear.

"What?"

"They are called love kisses. Those marks I wear some evenings when we are done."

"Oh, I did not realize. I shall try not to mark you again. It may cause problems…"

"Do whatever comes naturally to you. Harvey hides his blushes well when he shaves and dresses me."

"Oh, yes, Harvey." She had actually been thinking of the other woman in his life and how she would interpret those marks. "I had not thought of him. Poor man unable to make comments as to your person."

"He makes enough so that I know what he is thinking, but nothing too personal, I assure you."

The words between them were just that. Their minds and thoughts were on what was to come. Easing into the passion they would soon share.

"I understand, but what must he think?"

"He is not paid to think, so neither shall we."

He rubbed his ear against her palm when she stopped petting it.

She thought it best to return to her accounting of all his perfections. "And those shoulders —the muscles tapering to a slim waist. How do you stay so fit? Other men your age seem to have thickened in this area."

Leaning over he kissed her before answering. "I spar a little, but mostly it is from fencing and riding. In Italy I used to race over country roads pitting myself against others who thought they could out-pace Major and myself. It was exhilarating as well as good exercise."

"Hm-m-m." Sarah continued skimming her fingers over the curve of his waist to the more interesting of his body parts. The one that most intrigued her since it was so opposite her own. Opposite yet compatible. So much *yin yang* so to speak. His erection jerked when she dropped her fingers to rub across his lower stomach.

"May I touch it?"

Chuckling again, he answered, "Could I stop you? You may as well make yourself well acquainted with it since it is very acquainted with you—and what you like."

He glanced down his body and watched as she tentatively touched the soft crown and then followed a throbbing vein along one side. She stroked the staff and the soft sacks laying among the curls. "And this? I do not understand this part at all."

Seemingly unable to prevent his mouth covering hers as she tentatively held him, he pulled back explaining, "It's where my seed comes from. Be very careful of them."

"Oh, yes, I see where that makes sense. I shall be very gentle, then."

"They enjoy your touch. I enjoy your touch, but I think it is my turn to list the many parts I enjoy on you."

Blushing, she knew her entire body suffused with heat. He pulled himself away from her and scrutinized every part of her before saying, "I like your ears, too, but I do not think they are as sensitive as mine." He kissed one ear and then leaned away again as if seeking another area he particularly liked.

"Your neck, just here." He kissed the spot under her ear which always tickled when he did so. "And here. And here." With each word, he kissed a new spot on her neck heading down her body causing a tremble knowing where this was going. When he reached her sensitive breasts, he feasted before agreeing they were perhaps his most well-liked parts, but then continued to kiss down her stomach. He stopped, thankfully, when he reached her curl covered mound, and she sighed blissfully.

That is when he buried his face into her, and she felt the coolness of his tongue on her hottest spot. "Oh, Anthony, I, ah, I do not think…"

"Don't think. Simply feel. Let me do all the thinking right now. Relax and let it happen."

She did. She was past the point of being modest about any part of her body. Not with this man. This man who brought her such pleasure these past few weeks. The man who made her future so much easier, so much closer to the life she would have lived had Christopher married her, but this was not the time to think of him. She was experiencing a whole culmination of feelings which she knew led her to a pinnacle from which she would dive off and spiral to a climactic finish.

Panting, she realized she had grabbed Anthony's head at some point and had been stroking his ears encouraging him to bring her to fruition. Afterwards, he crawled up her body and laid his head next to hers. She had no words, but thought she should say something.

"That was wonderful, but I do not think you received the pleasure you usually seem to."

"I shall give you my seed before I leave," he

whispered, his gaze taking in her whole face moving from one part to another. His smile ever present.

"You are leaving Wyngate? I thought you planned on staying."

"There was a note waiting for me when I returned to my room. I have been called back for a day or two. I will not stay long, I promise."

"You do not need to promise me anything. If you wish to stay in London... I merely like to know so Cook can be informed. I will not expect you back until I see you."

He stared into her eyes as if trying to find another message there. As if trying to see if that was truly how she felt. He seemed satisfied with the answer he found.

"Do not get up to breakfast with me. I plan on leaving early, but I will not be gone long."

He put his leg over hers and entered her swiftly as if he could wait no longer for his own release. Bringing her to another orgasm, he then pushed into her pressing down for a minute or more before sighing and falling to the side.

"I shall miss this." He kissed her once more before getting out of bed and grabbed his robe, but merely held it in his hand as he left through the adjoining door.

Sarah watched the movement of his bare buttocks and smiled. If asked a month ago, she would never in a thousand years have thought this was where she would be at this time.

Rolling over to her side, she thought about his parting words. An odd thing to say to a wife taken only for the purpose of begetting an heir. She prevented herself from thinking about his mistress and what that woman would think of the words spoken so seriously moments before.

****

Travelling through the early morning fog as the sun warmed the earth and more of the world made itself visible, Tony could not stop thinking of the night before. He had not been prepared for what had occurred. How his wife lay there in welcome and how she touched him as if he was a new-found treasure. Her words, her touch inspired him. Inflamed him into doing something he had not done in years.

When had he stopped pleasuring Marguerite with his mouth? He knew he had wished to taste her, map her body with his lips when they were new lovers, but time and possibly propinquity had prevented him from continuing the experience. He remembered Marguerite had received pleasure, but then what? He got the impression his lover had not enjoyed the experience or wished to meet his own desire for such activity.

Last night, he was moved to reciprocate his wife's obvious pleasure in his body. When he began noting her body parts as she had his…the rest simply fell into place. It seemed so natural, so needed. It never hit him until this morning how much he had wished to taste her, to have her essence on his lips and tongue. He thought he could still smell her, and a smile crossed his face.

And Sarah had responded so very quickly and so very sensually. He could imagine her reciprocating with her sweet mouth on his hot body parts. Tasting and teasing until he could not prevent the inevitable conclusion. He felt his member begin to throb and knew he would be aching if he did not change his thoughts to less erotic images.

Concentrate on Marguerite and her possible

emergency so soon after his leaving her. How was he to build any kind of life with Sarah if he spent days visiting London and at this particular time? He was learning more and more about his wife and how much more she was than he had thought.

When he first returned to London, he was inundated with invitations to the finer homes. After all, his mother had put it about that he was in need of a wife. He even accused her of putting a notice in the newspaper announcing such.

Tony became reacquainted with speaking to debutants who had little to offer in way of conversation or ideas. Even knowing they were probably told by their mothers to agree with any gentleman no matter what his ideas, he had problems keeping up his end to the inane chatter most young women thought polite conversation. With his newly acquired title, he had been feted to every ball and evening event followed by dinner invitations to every home housing an unwed lady of marriageable age. He was polite while Marguerite became less and less so—to him anyways. She resented his abandoning her to seek her own entertainment. Her pouts and threats finally culminated in his decision to marry a woman such as he had. Someone who knew he had another woman who meant as much to him as any wife could, meant more to him, in fact.

That last part seemed to satisfy Marguerite's need for reassurance. He could understand her insecurity even if he found it unreasonable after all their years together. After all that he had given up to keep a relationship with a woman so many years older than himself. In Italy he had been thought of as a gigolo, at least at first. It was not as if there were not such men available in every large city, but it hurt his pride to be thought of as such a man. Besides, it was a slight to Marguerite and her beauty and delightful presence.

Eventually society realized he had his own money and spent it lavishly on his paramour, perhaps overly so to compensate for what others thought him to be. Marguerite preened in his attentions and thought the gifts he gave her were proof of his devotion and love. He knew she was waiting for the day he would say he was returning to England or even that he had found another woman. Perhaps that was why he made sure she never had a reason to doubt his adoration. Prove she never need fear he would leave her as she aged. He had been adamant their feelings for one another were stronger than the bonds ordinary people lived by. That he would remain faithful and true till death do them part.

A deep rut tossed the carriage from one side of the road to the other. Tony held onto the strap to steady himself on the bench seat. These trips needed to end. At least until Sarah was with child, but how could he accomplish that if he was always riding between Wyngate and London? He would have to emphasize his need to stay with his wife for a prolonged period of time. He would need to make it plain to Marguerite—right after he straightened out whatever emergency caused her to summon him from his home once again.

****

"Good morning, Cook. I thought I would make some chicken soup and take it around today since some of the villagers have come down with some sort of influenza."

"I thought you might, my lady, and I've had a couple of carcasses boiling since early this morning." Picking up the small plate saying, "I got your egg on toast right here."

The woman set it in front of Sarah.

Sarah took one look, one sniff then headed to the washbowl and tossed up her stomach's contents. "Oh, I am so sorry. I do not know what came over me." She wiped her mouth with the corner of a dish towel.

"I was the same way with my third. Could not abide the smell of eggs so for three months my man went without his mornin' victuals. Had to do with anything he could find."

"I may be with child, but I did not feel this way with the first…"

Sarah's gaze snapped to the round woman going about her tasks. Perhaps Cook had not been listening.

"I found each one's different," Cook continued. "Could not pass a dairy with the first and the second there did not seem to be anything I did not wish to eat— at any time."

Sarah remained quiet, unsure what her cook would make of things. The woman stopped and stared at her. "Here, my lady, try some dry toast. That always helped me." As she hurried to the larder she continued talking, "And don't worry that I shall be a sayin' anything, but no one can help knowing that Topher is yours no matter how much Lucy carries him around on her hip. Those hips have not birthed a baby yet—, but she'll be due about the same time as you, maybe a few weeks sooner."

"I was not trying to keep it a secret from you—not really. Lord Wyndom knows I gave birth but thinks my son died. I hid his existence from the grandparents so they would not come and take him from me. I was so young…"

"No need to explain anything to me, my lady. I think you are the best thing to happen to Wyngate in a long time, so if it's to be a secret, then that's what it'll be. I shall make sure the others know as well."

"They all know Topher is mine, then?" Sarah worried how she was going to face these kind people after keeping them in the dark about something so important. Kept it from their lord and master.

"As I says, it's right obvious to most o' us. Not that he takes after his mother, but it's more of how you are with him. A right proud mother while Lucy treats him as a loving aunt might."

"I guess I should tell Lord Wyndom before someone slips. I am not sure what he will do, but I wish everyone to know I appreciated how well I was received when I came here out of the blue. I wish everyone to remember that."

"I don't think you'll be going anywhere, my lady. After all, you may be carrying the next viscount, and that shall mean a whole lot, I am sure. The master has his heart set on a son sooner rather than later. He will not set you aside no matter what he thinks to do."

"Still, I do not want this hanging over my head—any of our heads. When the viscount returns home, I shall tell him the truth. Then we'll see how things go on from there. Lord Wyndom will not be remaining in residence much longer anyway."

Each morning, Sarah woke in this amazing place and lived a fulfilling life, and it was all due to the man she married. A man she worried about tying her life to. A man she worried would not understand her need to hide her own son to protect him from the possibility of being taken from her. Taken and given to people who may do no more than keep him fed—for a price.

The people who surrounded her now were such good people and ones she had betrayed with her deceit. Yet she knew they would, they had, accepted her need to do so. Had understood and were willing to keep her secret if she had, but asked them.

Sarah knew she was smiling and knew why. She had found the one man in this world who could replace the love she thought she had lost. The one man who made her heart sputter and skip beats. The one man she would be proud to claim as her husband and the father to her children. Even if he returned to Italy and the life he lived there, he was a man she could teach her children to respect for his loyalty, his honor, and for keeping his promises.

He was a man they would never need feel ashamed of no matter what they should hear. She would make sure they knew him as honorable, if unconventional. She would never feel stilted in any manner. If she returned to society or visited London, she would remain loyal to him no matter that he lived with another woman. Her husband deserved her loyalty just as she had told him when they first met.

At the time, she thought it was because she could never think of another man the way she thought of Christopher, but now she knew it to be more. Now she would never be with anyone besides Anthony because her heart had only been bruised. Her marriage mended it and made her stronger. Made her realize the difference between infatuation and true love.

Knowing Anthony and his kindness toward so many people, his need to treat everyone as well as he could, as honestly as he could, had her fall in love with him. His lifestyle would not have been her choice, but the life she lived now was more than satisfying. Her love would be cherished. Knowing she had made Anthony's life happier was more than enough.

****

Sarah sat back in the chair amazed at the information. "That is excellent news, Mr. Fellner. I was not expecting such a substantial amount for the tenants."

Sarah was impressed with the amount of funds to be returned to the tenants by way of coins. They had already released some of the stored crops to the tenants so they would have enough to make it through the winter and spring until crops would be harvested again.

"Lord Wyndom made it happen, my lady. Once he realized how dire some of them would be by next summer, he insisted we return what we still had and add funds to make up the difference.

She did not wish to think well of her husband right now. She needed to think of him as a protagonist in all of this, or she would feel even guiltier in keeping Topher's true relationship her secret.

"Mrs. Griffin and Mrs. Springstead have worked on a menu for Christmas Eve and Boxing Day. The entire village is invited for Christmas Eve before church service. We shall have seasonal foods, hot cider and ale, and special treats for the children. The tenants shall receive their coins then, and I would appreciate it if you handed those out."

"But will not Lord Wyndom wish to do so?"

"I believe Lord Wyndom shall be spending the holidays in town with friends."

She noticed the expression of pity that crossed his face and sighed inwardly. How did one explain that one did not expect their husband's attention on such days even if that same husband spent almost the entire night in one's bed?

Bowing, he said, "Then I accept the honor, my lady. Is there anything else you shall need of me?"

"Possibly to help Griffin pass out the gifts. I know he knows all the staff and many of their family members, but you are more acquainted with the tenants. The men's and children's gifts are all the same, but the women's are tagged with their name.

"My lady, I would like to lead the footmen out to collect the greens. I have been noting where holly and mistletoe are growing this year. Despite the poor rain early on in the year, those plants seemed to have weathered the drought better than others. The evergreen boughs as well."

"I do not want a yule log, but all the rest is a must." Sarah made notes on her list.

"As you wish, my lady. And Boxing Day…?"

"A special meal for all those working at the estate which includes the gardeners and stable hands. I think that shall be about seventy-five with spouses and other family members. The food shall be ready that morning, and Mrs. Springstead is seeing to volunteers to serve it. I, of course, shall do my duty as well."

"I don't think the staff really mean for you to do such a thing, my lady."

"No, no, it is the least of what I can do. After all, I do not have any place else to be. Nanny Wright shall be coming here as shall Mrs. Coop with Lucy and Topher. Everyone I care about shall be right here with me."

If the man thought that a strange comment, he kept it to himself. The holiday was as she had always planned it being. She would show hers and the viscount's appreciation for the work the tenants and the servants did. She would keep vigilant finding ways to increase crops and animal production, and she would be the best viscountess she could be as long as she was able.

She would also show her appreciation for the man who made it all possible, Lord Wyndom. She would bear him a child in less than eight months, hopefully the heir he wishes and the life she had planned for her and her children would be set. Lord Wyndom could leave for Italy, and she could move Topher into the house beside the new baby.

Lucy would be busy with her own child by then, so a new nurse and perhaps later a nanny would be hired for both her children.

Depending on his whims, Lord Wyndom would return to bless her with another child and then leave again giving her the freedom to raise her brood as she wished. It would be just as she planned and as Lord Wyndom had indicated he wished things. Except for Topher, she would live the life of a viscountess as her husband explained to her.

CHAPTER NINE

"Why is Lucy's son in the nursery?" Anthony asked as he passed the open door evidently seeking her out.

"Oh, ah, Lucy's mother, who usually watches the boy, is not feeling well so I told her to bring him here where it was safer. She is not sure that her mother doesn't have something the child could come down with. It would be a shame for him to be sick and then Lucy would stay home until he was well again. You know how much I depend on her for everything."

Sarah hoped her husband was not going to question her about what all those important things were that required Lucy to remain in the main house with her child rather than take a few days off to care for an ailing mother.

"He can be closer if that would help out things. I do not see that he would bother me even in the evenings. You know how deeply I sleep."

The expression he gave her was still questioning as if he did not quite understand her thinking.

"Lucy expects him to be in the nursery, and it is closer to the backstairs so any of the staff can come up and bring in meals and such. I think he should stay here since he is familiar with the room already."

Shrugging as if he did not care one way or the other, he left to change his clothes, and she sat in the rocking chair and watched her son sleep.

Topher's sweat-glistened forehead and the manner in which he tossed himself about was her first warning. He had not been sick since the first few weeks of his life, but this was different. As an infant he lay silently and piteously in his small cradle. Now he thrashed about winding the sheet about his plump body. His glazed eyes sought comfort and help from her.

"Oh, Topher, oh, my love, how can I help you?"

Sarah glanced toward the wash stand then went to wet a linen. She wiped her son's brow and neck trying to cool his body. She knew a temperature in a small child was normal, but she did not like the way he seemed unable to recognize her or where he was. The thrashing continued as she removed the damp night shirt allowing him to lay on the sheet uncovered.

Wishing one of the staff would arrive to check on them, she remained with her son, unwilling to leave him alone even for the short time it would take to get help. Besides, what could anyone else do? The doctor was out on house calls she was sure seeing to others who had been coming down with this same malaise all week.

She finally heard footsteps and sighed in relief. Someone she could tell to bring Cook or Mrs. Griffin to help. Both women had had children and might have more knowledge of how to treat such a fever.

Her husband's voice roared out from the doorway. "Why are you in here? Especially if the boy is ill? Call the doctor and have Lucy take the child home. I do not wish you becoming ill, not if you are possibly with child. Lucy should be here where she belongs."

"Lucy is where she belongs. She is taking care of her mother and I…I am taking care of my son." Standing as if a lioness protecting her cub, she dared the man she married to say anything against her doing so. "And the doctor has been called, but this fever has gone through the village like a wild fire. So far, no one has died although there are still many too sick to know if they shall pull through or not."

She wiped Topher's flushed skin again ignoring the astonished expression on her husband's face. This was not how she planned on telling him. In fact, she hoped she would never need to tell him until after she had given birth to at least one child for him. But this was her son, and she was the one to care for him no matter the cost to her or to her marriage.

She had not promised her husband not to love another child besides his. She had promised Topher she would never abandon him or leave him for any length of time. That promise superseded any and all others.

"Do you mean that you have been passing your own son off as Lucy's? Hiding the truth from me?"

"I was hiding the truth, for now, from everyone. An unmarried woman has no rights over her own child if the father's family should suddenly decide to claim him. I was afraid that once the Geoffrey's thought about things and recovered from the grief of their son dying, they would take my son as a replacement. I had offered them the place of being my child's grandparents, but at the time, they did not wish to sully their son's good name by assuming he had fathered a child onto an unwed woman. Even if I had the ring he gave me as proof he intended for us to wed."

"But this boy lived with Lucy."

His glare was hard as he stared at her then turned a softer expression toward her son lying in the crib.

She continued trying to relieve Topher's fever.

"I have visited my son every day since we moved here. He lived with me until he was weaned when he was nearly a year old. That is when I began to fear someone would come and take him. I was still under the age of majority, and I did not trust my own father not to wrench him from me and send him somewhere I could not find him. Instead, I wrote my mother saying my child had died, and I was never returning home so they need not search for me. To be honest, I think they were relieved. Only Godmother knew where I was staying."

"Ah, I did hire a Bow Street Runner who went through a lot of small villages as a tinker inquiring after any young woman fitting your description." He spoke as if to keep her mind from worrying although he seemed as worried as she was now. "Is there anything I can do? Hurry the doctor, perhaps?"

"No, but thank you for the offering. A sick child is all consuming, and I really do not wish to speak about this right now. If you could find something to keep yourself occupied, I would appreciate it."

He did not seem put out by her dismissal of him, but again she really could not take the time from worrying about Topher to caring what a healthy adult male did or did not do. Her husband could return to his mistress in London if he feared contracting the fever, and perhaps, she should have mentioned that as a possibility.

"I shall bring you a light meal with tea. Do you think some soup for your son, would help?"

"He has taken sips of tea from a spoon, but I do not think he would be able to do more. His head is so hot..." Worriedly she wiped the cool flannel over his too warm forehead again.

Athony's brows furrowed as he contemplated

possible treatment. He lightly touched Topher's skin. "He is so hot. Should we open a window and allow the cooler air to bring his temperature down? Perhaps bathe his entire body and allow the evaporation to cool his skin? It just seems like what should be done."

"I know he could go into convulsions if the fever gets too high. When that occurs the child often never improves."

She refused to allow fear to overtake her. She could not consider any thoughts other than that her son would recover. Her thoughts had to remain positive—for Topher's sake. To keep him with her.

"Then that is what we should do. I shall have a tub brought up, and we shall fill it with warm water and submerge his body. Then go from there."

Anthony turned back to the doorway and disappeared, but she could hear him waking the footman in the front hall and giving orders. Soon half the household were awake and aware of the small child ill in the upstairs' room. She also heard her husband refer to the child as her son more than once. Well, there would be no need for fabrication any longer. Both she and Lucy would be free to speak the truth with anyone now.

The burly footman brought in the bath, and then two maids brought up pails of water, asking if there was anything more they could do for the child.

"No, no, thank you. I am sorry to be such a bother so early in the morning."

"Oh, my lady, this is not a bother to us. We're glad to be of service and help the little one through this. I had heard there was illness in the village but was surprised it made its way to the main house."

One of the maids stopped to look at Topher. "He's

such a handsome boy."

Anthony appeared in the doorway saying, "Mrs. Springstead sent up some shallow bark tea and said to give him only a sip."

Topher began to thrash and gasp. Scooping up the toddler, Anthony lowered Topher into the cool water causing her son's eyes to snap open then close as he relaxed in the man's arms.

Grateful that Topher appeared as if he were no longer in such discomfort, Sarah used the spoon to get a small amount of the medicinal tea into her son. It took both their voices coaxing before Topher accepted the bitter brew, but Sarah thought it had gone down.

"I think we can dry him off and put him to bed. We will leave the water in case we need it again, but I hope this works. He looks so ill and helpless…"

Anthony lifted her son while Sarah wrapped the small listless body in a towel.

Hoping to get some relief from Anthony and waylay possible questions, she said, "I shall stay with him. You are tired from your day of travel and should rest."

"We shall both stay with him. That way one of us can run for anything he may need. I do not wish him left alone for even a moment." His gaze moved over the small figure tucked into the crib. "They are so small, aren't they?"

"He seems large to me, my lord. He started out so small and so ill. He did not begin to gain weight for weeks after his birth although I tried to coax him to nurse. His breathing had been affected during birth. He came early, and I worried every morning it would be his last."

"How was he cured that time?"

"He simply woke one day, and his eyes followed me when I moved. I knew he was going to live and become a sturdy little boy. I cannot tell you when or why, but my prayers and his strength pulled him through. He has not had so much as a cold since."

"Well, let us hope this time is as miraculous. There have not been any deaths in the village so perhaps this is something that works its way through the body and then leaves as quickly as it arrives."

"I pray it is so, my lord."

He glanced to her face and said, "Anthony. I love to hear my name on your lips and this little one shall need to know who I am. I will not be 'my lord' to him either."

Unsure what her husband meant by those words, she simply leaned against his shoulder and hoped Topher would keep sleeping peacefully until the fever passed.

Late the following afternoon, Topher woke and pulled on Sarah's gown saying, "Mine, mine."

"Yes, little one, Mamma is right here. I shall always be right here close-by."

Anthony woke from his sleep in the rocking chair where he had moved giving her more room on the cot next to her son. "Is he better? He sounds better."

"He seems fine. I would not have thought it would be so sudden, but it is almost like last time." A tear rolled down her cheek.

"I shall send someone up to watch him while you eat and change your clothes. Perhaps take a rest in your room."

Anthony moved catlike toward the door after checking on Topher as the baby crawled onto her lap now that she was sitting.

"I shall take a meal and some of that broth I know

Cook has simmering on the stove. Oh, and some bread. I shall dunk it for Topher to eat. Tea, but no milk, yet, I think."

As if expecting him to bulk at her directions, instead he nodded. "I shall have it sent up, but I wish you to rest if you can get your son to lay down again."

CHAPTER TEN

"Tony, you are becoming too involved in that woman's life. I agreed you needed a legitimate heir, and we decided you would take this woman who is no better than she should be and get her with child. Then we were to go on with our lives. I came to England with that in mind." Marguerite was both hostile and belligerent. Neither looked good on her, causing her mouth to droop and eyes harden.

"That woman is my legal wife and as such I feel obligated to help her. If I had known her child lived, I would have made the same arrangements. The boy must be protected if anything should happen to me just as my wife and the children we have between us, shall be."

Tony thought what he had done about securing an heir would have no bearing on his relationship with Marguerite and still was not sure how it did.

"But you are doing enough by feeding her and putting a roof over her head. Can you not see what people shall think? That you care for her more than you do for me. Possibly that the boy is yours also. People shall talk and ruin everything."

"Everything? For who? And as to people talking, perhaps you should have thought of that before you allowed Lord Avon to accompany you home after so many balls. And then have his carriage be seen picking him up the next morning."

Pouting, she batted her lashes at him. Why had he not seen that expression for what it was? A way to manipulate him as a young girl would, but on an older woman, the expression did not have the same appeal.

"I told you I was lonely and missed you. I warned you I was not going to stay at home night after night."

"And foolishly I thought that meant you would attend the functions you always have and come home—alone. I did not realize you wished an open relationship."

"But you had your little wife in the country while I had nothing. Lord Avon gets invited to all the *tonish* events that I wish to attend. He buys me jewelry and is not afraid to be seen with me."

"Evidently, if my friend's warnings of every time they saw the two of you together is anything to go by. I do not understand what happened between us? I married a woman willing to look the other way so we could remain together. Why could you not wait for just a while longer?"

Facing him, Marguerite yelled brashly, "I am not used to waiting for what I want. You were ignoring me, and I found someone who loves me for who I am. He does not pine for the younger version of myself. He only knows me how I am now, and it is good enough."

Those words shocked him into stopping his own complaints. Was that what he had been doing? Had getting a young wife and feeling her firmer form, her perfect skin, her body lush for making love made him mourn for the past? Had he turned from Marguerite after bringing her across a sea?

Shaking his head, he knew it was not true. "It is true I began to see you differently, but not due to comparing you to my wife. Not physically that is, but you have proven yourself to be selfish and immature and disloyal. You tell me anything I wish to hear while doing what you want behind my back."

She scoffed and turned away from him. Something she did when she felt her stand was slipping and she was losing an argument. The years together had taught him something.

He continued speaking calmly, "Marguerite, I allowed you your little flirtations because I know it made you feel beautiful and sought after. I understood your need to have younger men escort you to Venetian breakfasts and strolls in the parks or along the beach leaving me at home waiting for your return. I thought you understood my need for a wife and legal heir."

"The others, they meant nothing to me, Anthony, I promise you."

"I know that. I did not feel you disloyal for having a stream of young men at your beck and call. It has always been your way, but you never bedded them." The thought made him rethink his memories. "Or am I mistaken in that, also?"

"*Non*, I was not interested in them when I had a young man in my bed who could keep me well satisfied."

Tony took some comfort in her words, at least, though he was not sure why. Perhaps only in that he had not misplaced his regard and trust for longer than these past few weeks.

"So, things changed when we arrived on English soil? There is a chance for us if we return to Italy?"

He wondered if he could recapture the feelings, he thought they shared.

"*Non*, I had hoped there was, but you have changed here. You are not as fun. You dine with your friends at your club where I am not allowed. You wish to make sure we shall not run into your mother, or her sister, or your grandmother or the woman's godmother. So many people to hide from it gives my head an ache. I do not like this place."

"I can move you anywhere in the city you wish to live."

"It is not the house it is this place. This London. It is not sunny or warm enough to walk out and be seen. It has too many places where I feel unwanted and less than the *contessa* I am. I should be asked everywhere like I was in Italy. I wish someone to think I am the sun and the moon again as you once did. I like the way Lord Avon thinks of me."

"I see. And is Lord Avon willing to take you to the continent? Back to Italy?"

"I have asked him, and he seemed more than willing. He said he always wished to travel, but his wife never wanted to. She is now gone and that leaves us free to do so. I promised to show him the capitals of the world."

She no longer appeared saddened by what was occurring between them. Possibly just as he was accepting her leaving, but he needed to know he had not been a fool since the beginning.

"Would you have been sad if I had left Italy when I had intended after the first six months? Or would you have found another benefactor? A man with deeper pockets to spoil you in the manner you wished to become accustomed?"

He watched as she fussed with her negligee. "Oh, do not say such things, Darling. You know I loved you then. You were exciting and fresh and so in love with me…it was exhilarating."

"But not so much any longer? Is Lord Avon exhilarating?"

Her shoulders shrugged in the way he used to think charming and French, but now seemed like a sullen response.

"Has he other attributes that attract you? I mean besides the fact he has wealth and is willing to take you back to Italy immediately." He wished to hear there was more than sex between Marguerite and him. He wished to hear her admit there had been love. "Why did you stay with me, then? Why not simply send me on my way?"

"It is not simply the money although you know I no longer have any of my monies left to me by the *conte* upon his passing. When I first became a widow, I truly thought I would need to remarry. At my age and the fact I was barren meant it would need to be to a much older man. One not as, um, vigorous in his needs as you were."

"You are right. We were compatible then, and we filled one another's needs which I confess have changed—for me anyway. I am sorry I did not live up to my vow of being there for you forever."

"Do not worry overly much, Darling. A young man's vow is taken with a grain of salt as they say— especially by a middle aged *contessa* who wasted her youth on an old man. I forgive you for finding what everyone seeks."

He tipped his head in question. "What do you mean?"

Chuckling she drew her hand across his cheek as a mother might a young child. "Darling Tony, you love your wife, and I could not be happier for you. At least one of us has found true love and perhaps Lord Avon shall be that for me. A man who cherishes me and appreciates me for myself. We hold no illusions with one another, and I find that refreshing. I shall always be younger to him. Someone he thinks himself lucky to have won since he feels he has bested a much younger man for my affections."

Raising her hand, Tony pressed his lips to it. "I do not know if the man deserves you, but you deserve all the happiness you think he shall bring you. I shall say my goodbye now since it sounds as if the next time I am in town you shall already be back in Italy being hailed the conquering heroine with your wealthy earl in tow."

She smiled, staring into his eyes. "Be well and love often. I hope this wife of yours is what you wish her to be."

They parted with warm feelings between them, but not love, no longer love—if it had actually ever been there.

CHAPTER ELEVEN

Tony raced back to Wyngate. He tried to find the words he needed to tell Sarah he wished to change the agreement between them. That he had not realized how his emotions would change having someone like her in his life.

Taking care of her, of her son, had not been a difficult decision for him, after all. Once he met her in that cottage garden, he knew Sarah would be the perfect mother for his children. What he had not realized was how perfect she was for him. That she was what he had been missing all these years. Marguerite had been entertaining and diverting, but she had no substance. Marguerite's entire life had been about what she wished and what made her life easier. The *contessa* never actually thought about another soul, and that included Tony. He was the entertainment and diversion she craved. The novel plaything who danced to her tune and whom she showed off like some prize pig.

Why had he not seen the woman for what she was? Yes, she was beautiful. The loveliest woman he had ever met, and she complemented his wish to have a beautiful woman on his arm. Tony wished to be known as her lover and went out of his way to make sure everyone understood their relationship. That was in Europe. Here in London things changed.

Tony had not really wished to introduce her to his

friends. He had thought it was because he feared they would try to come between Marguerite and himself, but it was not that at all. He knew they would judge him by the woman at his side. While they had all married women of their own class and begun families, Tony had tied himself to an older woman not interested in a family or anything minutely associated with them.

Marguerite knew her own self much better than Tony had. He not only misjudged himself, he misjudged what he wished from life when it all came down to it. He thought he had willingly tied himself to Marguerite when, in fact, he wished for a very different life. He wished for the traditional life he grew up expecting.

Perhaps his parents were a little standoffish, but they made sure he had everything he needed plus that he was surrounded by people who cared for him and about him. The same ideals he looked for when searching for a mother for his children. A woman who put her child before herself. A woman who chose her child over her own family and the society that would condemn her for an ill-thought-out relationship.

Now he returned to convince that woman he had been mistaken as to what he wished—wished from her and for his family. Yes, he wanted a mother who would choose her children over anything else in the world, and he wanted a woman who would do anything in the world for him. With him. Love him and make babies with him until they are both too old to do so any longer.

****

Sarah had seen her husband drive away in the carriage the morning after Topher had been announced free of the fever. It was as if the viscount could not get away soon enough—even leaving without speaking with her. Without telling her of his plans to return or if he even was going to return. Perhaps finding her with a living son and caught in a blatant lie for the weeks they had been married had caused a change of plans. Made him rethink his commitment to getting a child upon her though he had already accomplished that duty. Of that fact she was now certain.

There were so many reasons for Sarah to admire the man she married. She liked the way he made sure his nanny was taken care of even after all these years, that he cared about making sure Billings kept his title and job even though the man was well past the time most would have put him out to pasture. She liked how he treated the aging Griffins and Mrs. Springstead's son who had severe afflictions after being kicked in the head by a horse at their last employer. Now the lad was much like a young child yet the viscount treated him with the same consideration he gave every tenant. Anthony had even given him a job in the stables working with the horses the young man still enjoyed. Those were some of the reasons she loved her husband…

Yes, loved. She could admit it and took solace in doing so. The truth made her feel she could allow their children to know their father as she did. Have them feel the same pride in being of his family that she felt. She could not say when it began—only that it is.

When she thought of her lieutenant, it was as if it happened a million years ago. And to another woman. A woman who did not understand how strong love truly was and how passionate one could feel about another. She had a mere taste of what love could be with her lieutenant while she found a bountiful cornucopia of desire and passion with her husband.

Not that she would ever allow him or others to know. They made an agreement, and she would die before she broke any one of the aspects. She would inform her husband she was sure she was with child and then prepare herself for his departure. Prepare herself to live in Wyngate as she had planned on doing. Loving the man she married was not such a burden to carry. She had lived with worse, and at least she would have part of him with her. She would have their child to love and care for alongside Topher.

At one point Sarah feared she could not stay. She was not sure how to explain it to Lucy and her mother, but Sarah felt she must do it on her own. She had to be strong enough to leave her husband taking his child with her and possibly never returning, never allowing this child to know a father either.

Various scenarios played in her mind. Pose as a widow? Perhaps more believable when one had two children in tow and in this time of war. Perhaps claim he was a sea captain who went down with his ship? Heroic and something no one could verify easily. Not if she did not give them reason to.

Upon more thought Sarah knew that was not what a man such as the viscount deserved. His honesty must be met with the same. She was Topher's mother and she would be the mother of the viscount's child as well. She would make it enough—for all of them.

Sarah made her way to the nursery where she could spend time with Topher. His baby chatter always soothed her, and she needed soothing. She needed something to calm this turmoil she had not been able to resolve. What she promised and what she felt she could do—two worlds so far from one another...

As she got nearer, she heard the rumble of a man's voice. Toby's? Had the man come to speak with Lucy about something? Could Lucy's mother be ill again? Hurrying through the partially opened door, she found her son and surprisingly her husband lying on the floor. A box spilled out miniature soldiers and horses while Anthony said, "Oh, no, those have pointy edges. Here chew this, that is what it is made for."

A soldier with an extended saber was removed from the tiny fingers and replaced with a smooth-edged silver chewing ring. Probably one Anthony had used at one time. Her heart softened at the vision they made together. One so dark and large the other so opposite.

How did she tell this man, who had fulfilled his side of the bargain so thoroughly, she was having second thoughts? Anthony had never caused her to regret her choice, had been generous to a fault for all her wishes to be met yet she thought of cheating him in the worst way possible.

She must have made a sound, for he turned his head to stare. "There you are. I knew you would show up here sooner or later. Instead of chasing through this large house I decided to stay put and wait."

"Um, where is Lucy?"

"I sent her away saying that you and I need to talk, and that I needed to learn more about my ward."

"Your what?"

Spinning into a sitting position facing her, he said calmly, "My ward. I have all the papers drawn up and from now on Christopher Jeffery shall be under my protection. He shall assume the same place in our family as our children except for the rights of inheritance which by law must go to my eldest male child. He shall be treated as a most loved son no matter what he decides to do in life. I added him to my will, and he is as protected as any of my legal children shall be."

Why had she worried about this man she married? From the beginning he had been honest about what he needed and what he wished of her. And she had not been as honest in return yet he still seemed to have forgiven her. In fact, he had acted in a much more honorable way than both sets of Topher's grandparents. They had wished to hush everything up and hide the child away. The viscount had made sure Topher was well and then went immediately to ensure the boy never got forgotten or pushed aside again. Made sure her son was as well-cared for as his own. She owed this man so much more than her loyalty and admiration.

Sarah wiped away the tears rolling down her face. "You did all this merely because you found out he was my child?"

He stood dusting his breeches giving her more time to compose herself. "Of course. Why would you think I would do anything less?"

"But I kept the knowledge of his presence from you."

"That did make me wonder what you truly thought of me, and then I remembered he had been hidden before we met so I did not take it personally. You had your reasons."

"I did not wish his grandparents taking him. Possibly putting him out to foster where I would never see him again."

"Well, that is an impossibility now. He is legally mine—ours as far as anyone else knows. He shall be the big brother for all the others."

"All the others, my lord?" She knew he was teasing her but found his words heartening. He would return to her at some point.

"Well, there is at least one on the way if I am not incorrect in my calculations. Then I thought in a couple of years you would allow me to give you another…"

"I wished to be sure before I told you. Told anyone. But then you left again." Her smile was genuine, and she let him see all her gratitude for what he had done. "The children shall keep one another company while you are away."

"Away? Where am I going?"

"Oh, I thought you wished to travel. Possibly return to Italy and the warmth of the Mediterranean."

"No, unless we go as a family." He raised her hand and played with the ring he had placed there a mere two months earlier. "I found a much stronger draw here in England. I found a woman who was generous with her body and her love. Who knows me better than I know myself. Who drives me to fits both in and out of bed."

"My lord, I do not under…"

His mouth covered hers and the last cognoscente thing she remembered was Topher's baby chatter at her feet. After several minutes Anthony allowed her to lean back, but she was rather breathless.

"I am still unsure of what you are telling me, husband."

"I have never been my best with words. I am more of an action sort, but since I sent Lucy away, we have a little one here who needs us to watch over him."

"Yes, he is quiet now, but not so much if I were to leave. Not now he has seen me."

Sarah was shy in this man's arms. This man who had

shown her how wonderful love was, how wonderful loving someone was.

"We'll simply sit here with him then, and I shall try to wait until he tires." Appearing alarmed, Anthony asked, "He does still take a rest in the afternoon, does he not?"

"Yes, he will tire out and have a light meal before being put down for a rest."

Her husband nuzzled her neck. "Is there any reason his parents cannot take a rest also?"

Smiling as he tickled her by sending warm puffs of breaths over her skin she whispered, "None that I can think of."

"Then I look forward to his taking that promised nap."

Anthony continued kissing her neck sending chills down her spine. She could not imagine what had gotten into him, but to alter his life and plans for them seemed a momentous decision made in a seemingly short time.

"I do not wish to harp on a subject that I vowed to stay away from, but what of your other plans? The agreement…"

His mouth covered hers, and she fell into the mesmerizing lure of his lips and tongue and the urgency he expressed.

Finally allowing Sarah a moment to recover, he whispered, "I am no longer obligated by any promise or vow other than the ones I gave you in front of the bishop. I was mistaken in my wishes and most assuredly in my needs. I am no longer that young foolish man more interested in the hedonistic lifestyle of certain continental courts. What I thought to be my future, my life, was right here in England beside my wife whom I found I love beyond words."

"You do? Are you sure?"

"Dearest, I have sent the other on her path. With a new lover, by the way, so I shall not be missed. I regret the time it took me to realize what I had here in my home. How much I yearned for you and this way of life whenever I was called away. I made excuses to myself, to others, but it was due to you, my dearest love. I wished to be by your side not acting the rake in London staying up all night gambling and drinking. I wish you, this home you have made for me and the children of your body. All the children born of your body."

His glance moved to Topher who appeared to have nodded off.

Lucy knocked and said, "I thought Topher would need his lunch about now. Then I shall remain nearby to listen as he sleeps."

Blushing, wondering how much her friend had seen or heard, Sarah nodded and with their hands clasped together, she and Anthony left the room.

Whispering as her bed chamber door closed, he said, "I wish to kiss you all over. Over and over. Strip you naked and kiss every part. Mark you as mine forever."

Sarah felt his need press into her stomach as she agreed.

"I wish that, too. I am practically shaking with need."

"Is it safe to do more, do you think? I mean with the baby…" His hand brushed across her lower stomach, and she accepted his kiss as well as the possessive touch.

"Yes, we can continue loving one another for months yet."

He stopped, and she heard his heavy breathing

wondering what stopped his lovemaking.

"Do we? I mean, love one another. I know how I feel, and we are married so that ties you to me, but how do you feel? About me, I mean."

Relaxing into his strong body she smiled. "I have loved you almost since the beginning. I love the way you cared for me. For making me comfortable in this life, in your bed and arms. I thought I knew what love felt like, but I did not. The emotion I felt for my lieutenant was a young girl's first infatuation. What I feel for you, my husband, is so much more. Is so much stronger and so much more a part of me."

Placing her head against his chest listening to his heart beat she admitted, "I was not sure how I was going to live if I needed to leave here. To protect Topher. He would be the only reason I would have left."

"I know that. Why do you think I stayed near him? I knew you would not go too far without him. I wished to be sure you took me with you, too."

"Silly man. I would not even have contemplated leaving if I had known your plans for us."

"The plan is to live in this beautiful home you made me. To raise a passel of children. To love my wife, thoroughly, for the rest of my life. Does that match with your plans?"

"Yes, all of them. Shall we begin as we mean to go on?"

"My pleasure, lady wife."

Anthony swept her into his arms and carried her to the open bed.

A word about the author...

A voracious reader her whole life, author Susan Payne loves the written word. When reading more than fifty books per month wasn't enough, she decided to allow her mind to take flight and write all the many stories that kept intruding in her life. She blended her love of history and her love of words to create over eighty stories. All historical and centering on a couple finding love and a happy ever after together. www.authorsusanpayne.com

www.ingramcontent.com/pod-product-compliance
Lightning Source LLC
Chambersburg PA
CBHW070510260626
47161CB00004B/1508